PRAISE FOR BARRY FORBES

AMAZING BOOK! My daughter is in 6th grade and she is home-schooled, she really enjoyed reading this book. Highly recommend to middle schoolers. *Rubi Pizarro on Amazon*

I have three boys 11-15 and finding a book they all like is sometimes a challenge This series is great! My 15-year-old said, "I actually like it better than Hardy Boys because it tells me currents laws about technology that I didn't know." My reluctant 13-year-old picked it up without any prodding and that's not an easy feat. *Shantelshomeschool on Instagram*

Great "clean" page turner! My son was hooked after the first three chapters and kept asking me to read more... Fast forward three hours and we were done! *Homework and Horseplay on Amazon*

This is Nancy Drew collaborates with the Hardy Boys. There are enough twists and turns to remind you of driving on Fish Creek Hill. ... Take a break, wander away from the real world into the adventurous life of spunky kids out to save the world in the hidden hills of the Southwest. *Ron Boat on Amazon*

A superb and rip-roaring mystery read, and good clean fun! Forbes nails it, and I'm looking forward to the rest of the series. *Arizona customer on Amazon*

Virtues of kindness, leadership, compassion, responsibility, loyalty, courage, diligence, perseverance, loyalty and service are characterized throughout the book. I recommend all elementary and junior high school libraries should have a copy of this book. *Lynn G. on Amazon*

THE VANISHING IN DECEPTION GAP

A MYSTERY SEARCHERS BOOK

BARRY FORBES

THE VANISHING IN DECEPTION GAP

A MYSTERY SEARCHERS BOOK

VOLUME 6

By
BARRY FORBES

ST. LEO PRESS

The Vanishing in Deception Gap © 2020 Barry Forbes

DISCLAIMER

Prescott, the former capital of the Arizona Territory, is considered by many to be the state's crown jewel. Aside from this central Arizona locale, *The Mystery Searchers* series is a work of fiction. Names, characters, businesses, places, events, incidents, and other locales are either the products of the author's imagination or used in a fictitious manner. Any resemblance to actual persons, living or dead, or actual events is purely coincidental.

Read more at www.MysterySearchers.com

For Linda,
whose steadfast love and encouragement
made this series possible

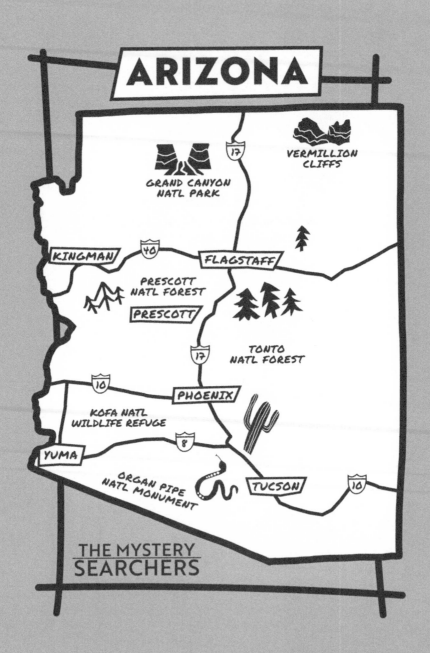

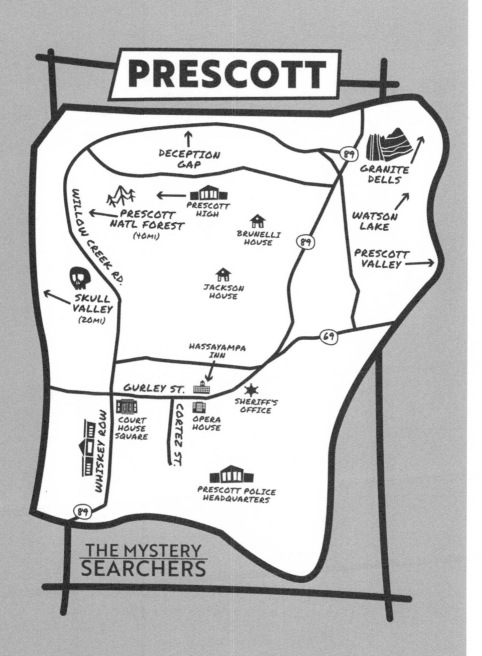

PURSUIT

Suzanne lay flat atop a steel-bodied boxcar, insulated from the cold metal by a light jacket, jeans, and running shoes, stomach down and churning, her eyes peeking over the rim as she gasped for breath. Her heart thumped, and even in the chilly early morning—it was after 1:00 a.m., a Thursday in late August—she felt clammy and hot. Sweat soaked her forehead and stained her clothes. A breeze sprang up from nowhere, passing over and around her before dying in the night.

Something her father, Edward Jackson—*Chief* Edward Jackson of the Prescott City Police—often said popped into her mind: "Stick to it, like chewing gum on the sidewalk. Never give up." The thought forced a weak smile. *I am, Dad. And I won't.*

From Suzanne's vantage point, snaking out in front she could make out dozens of boxcars, shadow-like shapes lit by dimmed LEDs and a full moon in a cloudless sky. They sat in a stationary line, harnessed together and prepared for a morning journey out of Deception Gap Railroad Yard. The train would depart at daybreak, on the way to Denver, Colorado, with a two-hour layover in Cheyenne, Wyoming. Loaded with freight from East Asia. Valuable freight too.

Final destination: New York City.

The immense line of boxcars extended northward before angling toward the northeast and fading into deeper shadows. Not surprising, really: the railway yard lights—capable of lighting up four hundred acres with a flip of a switch that turned night into day—had shifted to minimum power at the stroke of midnight: the light had faded by a good ninety percent. Far ahead, she knew, at the front of the line, out of sight, sat two giant locomotives. The mystery searchers—that was the nickname that the local press had given Suzanne, her brother, Tom, and their best friends, Kathy and Pete Brunelli—had passed the locomotives just minutes before: huge, iron beasts ready to roll, pulling the ninety-some boxcars behind them.

The boxcar Suzanne clung to stood at the back of the train. *Dead last,* she thought with an ironic grimace. She didn't dare move a muscle. No telling how close *they* were, but her mind all but screamed: *What happened to Kathy? Did the boys escape? Where are those evil men?*

And, moments later: *What was that sound?* Whatever it was—*A man coughing?*—faded in seconds. Still, there were no answers. Not yet. Just an unnerving silence that drove Suzanne's imagination into overdrive.

The next boxcar blocked her view in front. Suzanne pushed herself up higher but still couldn't see much. No visible fence surrounded the remote property—Deception Gap lay deep in the middle of nowhere. The terrain before her, she knew, was prairie flat and wide open: nothing but twin sets of steel tracks, one endless pair after another, with nowhere to hide. There wasn't even a good-size rock until a hill emerged to the east, climbing up and out of the natural basin that surrounded the railyard.

From her elevated perch, however, Suzanne had a sweeping view of the railyard's facilities. To her left—to the northwest, a couple hundred yards away—a four-story roundhouse, a huge relic from another century, dominated the railyard. Narrow bands of yellow light seeped out from the structure's massive front doors and filtered through banks of grime-covered glass panes. No way had those windows seen a wet rag in years. The monster building operated twenty-four/seven, every so often belching smoke into a starry night, and capable—so the mystery searchers had learned—of servicing multiple locomotives at one time. An intermittent *bang, bang, bang!* of steel hammering steel pounded out from somewhere deep inside the structure, penetrating the stillness. The roundhouse —named, Suzanne knew, for the gigantic floor-bound turntable inside—could rotate a locomotive 180 degrees with ease. She wondered what ungodly noise *that* would make when it was in operation.

There was plenty of danger there too. The Brunellis had discovered that on a previous foray. *The hard way.*

Next to the roundhouse perched the four-story control tower—lightless, foreboding, and deserted for the night. The tall, spindly tower, located at the exact center of the railyard, overlooked a ragged row of about a dozen small one- and two-story workshops stretching north to south: toolsheds, a foundry, and four buildings that appeared to have lain untouched for decades—squat structures built of stone and well over a hundred years old and all, Suzanne knew, locked securely.

The foursome had split up just minutes earlier, Suzanne and Kathy exploring on one side of the tracks, Tom and Pete on the other. They had walked straight into a trap. A gang of four masked men had materialized from nowhere on both sides of the train, yelling at the mystery searchers, cursing, and swinging metal bars. Despite their masks, Suzanne felt certain she had recognized one of the horrible men—something about his musculature, the way he moved. *It had to be him.*

In the melee—separated from their sisters, not knowing where or how to reconnect with them—Tom and Pete had vanished. Suzanne assumed they had fled north, surely their fastest and safest avenue of escape. Trapped by two men, the girls had bolted in the opposite direction.

Seconds later, Kathy tripped, perhaps on one of the tracks or a railroad tie. Or maybe a pursuer had grabbed her. *Who knows?* Suzanne thought. As she tumbled, Kathy had shrieked, "Run, Suzie, *run!*"

Suzanne did, as if the devil himself were after her. She stayed ahead of her two pursuers, hopping between boxcars from one side to the other, even rolling under one before sprinting away without ever looking back until—

Quiet descended abruptly. The only sounds Suzanne could hear were running footsteps and gasping breath—both, she realized, her own. The pursuers appeared to have given up the chase. She reached the back of the train, scrambled straight up the last boxcar's ladder, and dropped onto the flat roof, pasting herself against the steel surface, trying desperately to control her breathing and still her pounding heart.

Not—liking—this, she thought, replaying in her mind the *whoosh* of a steel bar swinging past her head. How had it missed her? She shuddered, attempting to regain control of her emotions, aware that her anger, an old nemesis, could mislead her into acting rashly. She heaved a deep breath. Only then did she reach for the cell phone in her jeans' back pocket.

It's not there! She groaned out loud. *Oh, Lord. It must have fallen out as I ran.*

Suzanne inched over to the ladder and glanced down, thirteen feet from the top of the boxcar to ground level. In the shadow cast by the moonlit train, it was impossible to see anything. She hesitated. *Now what?* A light flashed twenty feet farther up the track. *My phone! On mute, thank God.* Someone was calling.

Suzanne flung her legs over the side and clambered down the ladder, paying no heed to the danger. She raced up and grabbed her cell phone, her heart bursting with joy. *Tom Jackson,* the screen read, beside a close-up of her twin brother's smiling face. *You've never looked so good.* She jabbed the screen with one finger and ducked under a boxcar, crouching behind its giant wheels.

"Tom, where *are* you?" she demanded in a hoarse whisper.

His anxious relief poured out. "*Suzie!* We've been calling you. We made it to the locomotives. No one followed us. Are you both okay?"

"I am, but I think they caught Kathy."

"What?" Pete blurted in the background, his voice rising with alarm. *"They grabbed Kathy?"*

"I think so. She tripped or something and yelled at me to keep going. I outran them."

Tom considered what his father would have to say. It wouldn't be pleasant. "Where are you now?"

"I'm hiding under the second-last boxcar. Those horrible men can't be far away." She hesitated. "What would they do with Kathy?"

"Let's meet halfway," Tom said, thinking fast, "on the east side of the boxcars."

"Got it."

"And don't get caught!" Pete snapped in the background. "That's the last thing we need."

"I hadn't planned on it," Suzanne retorted. She disconnected and poked her head out. All quiet. *Whoa. Wait a sec.* She touched the fitness app symbol on her screen—it would track her every step and store the data online, in the Cloud. *Just in case.* Then she rolled away and stood, listening once more, before retracing her steps alongside the boxcars, trying her best not to make a sound.

Meanwhile, the boys deserted the relative safety of the lead locomotive's cabin. They dropped to ground level and trekked along, slow and steady, alert against the first hint of danger.

At one point, Pete broke the silence, rasping, "We gotta rescue Kathy, and soon too. If we can't find her, we need to call for reinforcements."

"All we can do now is keep going. Suzanne should be close."

Moments later, a man's voice drifted their way, seeming to hang in the breeze. Laughter rang out. Two men. The boys slipped under a boxcar, waiting until the threat had melted away. Loud banging started up, a now familiar drumbeat.

By now, they figured Suzanne had to be getting close.

Somewhere a woman screamed, unleashing a shattering wail that pierced the night before it abruptly cut off!

"What the heck!" Pete blurted, grabbing Tom by one shoulder and bringing them both to a standstill. "Was that—?"

The boys broke into a run, hoping against hope that Suzanne was just seconds away.

2

NO REPLY

F our days earlier, a strange text message had arrived on Kathy's cell phone.

The four friends had just walked away from their final meeting at Daisy Hutchinson's stately Victorian home. It was late on Sunday afternoon, and a mountain summer storm had completed its handiwork, leaving puddles of water to negotiate on the way out to the car. Hours of drizzling rain from dark and dreary clouds had all but come to a halt.

Still, nothing could dampen the spirits of the mystery searchers. Their most recent adventure, the treasure of Skull Valley, had reached a successful conclusion, its loose ends tied into a tidy little bundle—and a joyful one, at that.

"With a bow on top," Kathy chimed. She was the one with the ever-ready sense of humor. The message had arrived an hour earlier —*ding!*—but she refused to interrupt the celebration. The nonstop, infectious laughter was *way* too much fun.

As they strolled out to the car, Kathy touched her Messages icon, and the fateful missive popped up on her screen. "Oh, wow, check it out."

She read the text out loud: *Pirates are operating out here and they're dangerous. I can't prove it, not yet, but I need your help. Please call asap.*

"Pirates?" Pete exclaimed, rubbing his hands together. Thunder rolled somewhere in the distance. "Nice. Very. I like it."

Suzanne tossed her head. The phone number had a local area code. "Whoever heard of pirates around here? That's ridiculous. We're four hundred miles from the ocean."

"No clue," Tom said. Quiet and thoughtful, he shared certain traits with the twins' widely admired father, one being the conviction that you should think first before opening your mouth. He searched Kathy's face. "You know this guy?"

"Beauford Bradley?" His name appeared over the message, together with a phone number. "Heck, no. Never heard of him. But he sounds desperate, doesn't he?"

Pete chortled. "*Beauford?* What kind of a name is that? And if you don't know him, how did he find your phone number?"

"You should never make fun of someone else's name," she retorted, her eyes flashing. "I imagine he spotted my number in *The Daily Pilot.* Most people would consider that rather obvious."

Prescott's hometown newspaper had run a final front-page article about the treasure of Skull Valley. The story featured an image of the online notice, created by Kathy, that had blown the case wide open. Kathy's phone number had appeared—in error, the photo editor had meant to blur it—all but indiscernible at the bottom of the screen capture.

Pete shrugged. Nothing Kathy ever said seemed to bother him. He considered bickering a sport that required a winner—him—and a loser—her. Besides, the brother and sister were exceptionally close; as a rule, they got along well.

The two sets of siblings stood beside the Brunellis' Mustang, hashing over the unusual text. They couldn't have appeared more different if they tried. The Brunellis were Italian through and through, a trifle shorter than their best friends, with coal-black hair and olive-hued skin. Pete and Kathy even looked alike, if not as much as the Jacksons, who were, after all, fraternal twins.

8

The Jacksons were both tall and willowy, with fair skin and brown hair.

Still, as Kathy often said, "Our personalities are as different as day and night."

Pete, for example, was known as the impatient one. "Let's roll. What's next?"

"Okay, just call the guy," Tom urged.

"Go for it," Suzanne said.

Kathy touched the number. No answer—the call went straight to voicemail: "Hi, it's Beau. Leave a message." *Beeeep.* She did. "And he calls himself Beau," she informed the others.

"Whatever," Pete said. He licked his lips, a sure sign of his legendary appetite. "Food—let's eat. Try him again later."

That evening, Kathy called again a few times. And the next day too, starting early in the morning. No answer. And no return calls. Ever. Straight to voicemail. "I'm worried," she declared, and not for the first time, glancing over to her brother at the breakfast table.

"Worry doesn't help anyone," Pete said, spreading gobs of smelly peanut butter on a slice of toast. He had just quoted their mother, Maria, an emergency room nurse at Prescott Regional Hospital, who had loads of experience dealing with worry. He licked peanut butter from his fingers. "Besides, Bradley's problem might have fixed itself. That happens."

"It sure didn't sound like that kind of problem," Kathy argued. She looked at him with disdain. "Your manners stink. How many pieces of toast have you eaten?"

He grinned. "Not enough."

She scanned the message for the umpteenth time. "I think this guy's in big trouble."

"I think you've got an active imagination."

"Shut up."

Their father, Joe, wandered in and out of his home office, half listening to the siblings' banter, catching bits and pieces. He sometimes liked to pace as he worked. As the founder and editor of a popular magazine that focused on world history, he had garnered a vast audience on the Web. "Why not search for the guy online?" he suggested.

Pete replied, "We did, Dad."

"And?"

"Zippo."

Beauford Bradley didn't appear to have any digital presence, although there were Beau Bradleys galore, all over the place. But none living, or claiming to live, in Arizona—at least not on Facebook, Instagram, LinkedIn, Twitter, WhatsApp, and half a dozen other lesser-known social-media sites. A Google search came up empty too. And in Prescott, there was no landline belonging to a Beauford *or* a Beau Bradley.

"I wonder if the guy was ever even born," Kathy grumbled.

Later, the mystery searchers agreed they had hit a dead end. "Could be a hoax," Suzanne concluded. "All we can do is wait."

3

THE VANISHING

Tom perused the Tuesday morning edition of *The Daily Pilot* over cornflakes, toast, and coffee. The twins' father had left an hour earlier on a police emergency. Their mother, Sherri—a social worker who worked from home—had yet to appear. An article on page three caught Tom's attention.

His head snapped up. "Hey, Suzie!"

Suzanne was upstairs combing out her long, auburn ponytail. "Hey, what?" she called back.

"There's a story in the newspaper on a missing guy, and you'll never guess who."

She raced down the stairs and into the kitchen. "Try me."

"Beau Bradley."

"You're putting me on." She grabbed a bowl from the cupboard and peered over her brother's shoulder. Above the article was a photograph of a pleasant-looking African American man in his late twenties wearing an open-necked shirt, clean-cut, with short black hair and an enormous smile. The headline read, "Missing man leaves no trace."

"No wonder he never returned our calls," Suzanne said, replaying his text message in her mind. "Is it possible he's on the run?" That was familiar language for the daughter of the chief of police.

Her brother replied between mouthfuls. "Who knows? He showed up at work for the afternoon shift and disappeared a couple of hours later. No one's seen him since."

"Where'd he work?"

"At Deception Gap Railroad Yard, just north of the city . . . in that huge roundhouse, I'd guess. He's a welder."

"Or *was* a welder." A frown crossed Suzanne's face as she poured herself a coffee and added lots of cream. "Remember that strange reference to 'pirates' . . ." It wasn't a question. "When did he disappear?"

Tom scanned the article. "Two days ago."

"What? *Wait.* Two days ago?" She sat down at the table and reached for the milk. "That would be Sunday, the same day he messaged Kathy. Around four in the afternoon. When was he last seen?"

Tom's cell phone buzzed. "It's Pete. Hey, bro." He put the call on speaker.

"Hey, yourself," Pete replied. "Did you see the morning paper?"

"Did we ever," Suzanne called out. "No wonder Beau Bradley hasn't returned our calls. The poor guy vanished!"

Pete was a perennial doubter. "Vanished? Heck, more likely he jumped on a train and headed out of Dodge. I mean, *come on.* Nothing could be simpler. The guy *works* there."

"No way," Kathy said, pushing into the conversation. "He messaged me at four p.m. and disappeared three hours later. They must have freaked him out, and that's why he tried connecting with us. It was an act of desperation."

"Creepy," Suzanne said. "When you say, *they,* who—"

"The pirates, of course," Pete cut in. "I mean, that's what the message said."

"You're being rude," Kathy reprimanded her brother. "Did you see who wrote the article?" she asked the twins.

"Never thought of looking," Tom replied, leaning into the newspaper. "Hey—it's none other than our friend Heidi Hoover."

"Whatever happened to the poor guy," Suzanne said, "can't be good. I mean, like, this is serious stuff. I'll bet the pirates *knew* he knew."

"It points to one thing," Tom deduced. "They mur—"

"Bumped him off," Pete interrupted again. "That's what you were thinking, right?"

"Right. And let's define 'pirate.'"

"A plunderer," Suzanne said. "Someone who robs or steals."

"Typically on the high seas," Kathy added.

"But not always," Pete said. "The word transfers to land too. Think of software pirates."

Suzanne's cell phone dinged with an incoming text message. "Guess who? Heidi's got perfect timing."

"What's she want?" Pete asked.

"Us."

THROUGH A HANDFUL OF CASES THAT THE MYSTERY SEARCHERS HAD solved, Heidi Hoover—*The Daily Pilot's* star reporter—had emerged as one of their best friends. Her coverage had often helped to push a case forward, and she never failed to splash the news across the front page. Once she had even shared in the reward money. And, in the secret of the mysterious mansion, her quick-witted intervention had led to the foursome's rescue.

Heidi was a few years older than her young detective friends, having graduated from their high school four years earlier. She was a short, cute, youthful woman with bouncy black curls and a dynamic personality. She had grown up in Prescott after her family had arrived as refugees from Mozambique. Now, many years later, Heidi was living her dream, racing from one news story to another.

"Grab a seat," Heidi said, greeting the foursome as they descended upon the newspaper's glass-enclosed conference room just an hour after she had messaged them. Her words shot out rapid-fire: clearly, she felt there was not a moment to waste. "I'm assuming you read my story on Beau Bradley, right?"

Heidi always drew a smile from Suzanne. The plucky, gung-ho reporter had a certain air about her, a personable charisma that drew people to her—an asset for an investigative reporter. "Did we ever," Suzanne replied. "So the poor guy just vanished?"

"Most certainly did," Heidi replied. "And that's more than strange from my perspective. Something's going on out there . . . and whatever it is, it's not good."

Tom tried reading her face. "When you say *strange* . . ."

"Well, Deception Gap railyard is a big place, but it's not *that* big. For example, there's only one road in and out, with its own security camera, right by the parking lot." A quizzical expression crossed her face. "Guess what? On the security discs, we spot Mr. Bradley arriving for work in his car before three in the afternoon, right? But here's the thing. He never leaves. Ever. Know what that means?"

"Sure," Pete said. "It means he caught a train out there, or they bumped—"

"Or he went nowhere," Kathy said, shooting her brother a disapproving glance. "Heidi, Mr. Bradley messaged us at four p.m. on Sunday, the same day he disappeared. Check this out." She passed her cell phone across the table.

"Wow, oh wow!" Heidi exclaimed as she read the text message. "*Pirates.* So I was right. I could sense the weirdness out there. Someone's lying. It's possible this guy is deader than a doornail."

"Are there other cameras out there?" Tom asked.

"Nope," Heidi replied. "The place is way north on 89, remote and off the beaten path. Until now, they've never had a problem that required additional security—or so they say." She stopped for a few moments to reread the message. "This is proof positive he figured his life was in danger. Have you talked to Detective Ryan?"

"Not yet," Pete replied. "That'll be our next stop."

"Well," Heidi said, "he tipped me off to get newspaper coverage on Mr. Bradley—that's where I got the story. The guy's landlady contacted Prescott City Police. Beau had failed to return home on Sunday night. She flipped out, claimed he's as reliable as a clock; no way would he just disappear. What's odd is that the railyard's management hadn't bothered calling anyone."

"Did they say why?" Suzanne asked.

"Oh, sure. People come and go all the time. It's not unusual for a worker to walk away without a by-your-leave. I get that—it happens here at the newspaper too, once in a long while." Heidi's eyes flashed as she leaned forward. "But here's why that story makes little sense: Beau Bradley worked at Deception Gap Railroad Yard for two years. He had built up overtime, vacation pay, and a retirement account with a couple grand in it. No way would he leave without saying adios."

"Unless he *couldn't* leave," Tom said. Silence enveloped the room.

Heidi leaned back and cradled her chin in her hands, scenes and snippets of conversation obviously playing through her mind. "Yup. Right on. The police located his car in the parking lot. I was there when they used a slim jim to open one of the car doors. He had tucked his wallet, including his ID and sixty-five bucks, into the glove box. And his dinner—two turkey sandwiches, an apple, and a bag of Doritos in a paper lunch bag—was lying on the front seat."

"No way did he jump on a train," Kathy surmised. A murmur of assent rose from around the table. "He packed a lunch—he hadn't planned on going anywhere."

"You got that right," Suzanne said, nodding her head. "He wouldn't leave that stuff behind, no matter what."

"Especially those Doritos," Pete said with a wicked grin.

"You *have* to do something about that stomach of yours," Kathy quipped, convinced her brother was half-serious.

"On the run, Beau would need cash, ID, credit cards, and food," Heidi declared, "none of which he took with him. You know what that means?"

"It means—he's dead," Suzanne said, almost gagging on the words.

"My conclusion exactly," Heidi said. "But I need proof. That's where you guys come in."

"Now you're giving me goosebumps," Kathy complained.

"Proof?" Tom asked. "Such as . . . ?"

"A body," Heidi declared, her expression serious. "Beau Bradley never left Deception Gap railyard—not alive, at any rate. Someone knows what happened to him. Who did the deed? For what reason? And where did they hide the poor man's remains?"

A shiver ran up and down Kathy's spine.

4

THE HUNT BEGINS

Detective Joe Ryan chuckled. "So Heidi tipped y'all off, huh?" he said, his southwestern drawl rolling lazily off his tongue. "I figured she might. Those guys at Deception Gap sent her for a loop, and that's not easy to do. That girl is sharp."

The mystery searchers had found Detective Ryan at the downtown police station just after lunch. A shortish individual of little hair and fewer words, the detective wore his trademark rumpled suit without the jacket, a long-sleeved blue shirt, and tie—as usual, there was a tiny notebook and pen sticking up from his shirt pocket —and scuffed loafers.

The man the Chief had often called "the best investigator on the force" had agreed to an impromptu meeting.

"Good timing," he said as they stepped into a sizeable conference room. He dropped the remains of his lunch into a paper bag and slid it beneath his chair. "I had a police car pick up Mr. Bradley's mother from the airport. She's on her way to see me now." He glanced at his watch. "Should be here in a few."

"We're about to meet a very worried woman," Suzanne said, her eyes downcast.

"Yes, we are," the detective replied, shaking his head. "But an accomplished woman too. She's the top realtor at a large Philadelphia firm."

"So that's where she's coming from?" Kathy asked. "Philadelphia?"

"Uh-huh, with a plane change in Phoenix. Her son grew up and attended school in Philly. She was a single mom and Beau's her only child." He stopped. "Or was."

"Well," Kathy said, "this will interest her." She pulled out her cell phone and searched for Beau Bradley's text. "We received it last Sunday at four p.m." She passed the phone to the detective.

He scanned the message before emitting a low whistle. "Did you know this guy?"

"Nope," Pete replied. "Never heard of him."

"*The Daily Pilot* ran the story about our Skull Valley adventure," Tom explained. "It included a screenshot of the online post we made."

"You could just make out Kathy's phone number," Pete said. "That's how he found us, we feel sure of it."

"Found *me*," Kathy corrected him.

The Chief wandered into the meeting. "Hey, what brings you downtown?" The foursome brought him up to date.

The twins' father scanned the message before turning to his lead investigator. "This case is trickier than we thought. It's an odd one, isn't it?"

"You bet it is. Railyard management presented a good show, but something felt off. I couldn't put my finger on it." The detective turned to Kathy. "He sent the message to you at four and disappeared three hours later. That's a heck of a coincidence, isn't it?"

"You're not kidding," she replied. "Whoever the 'pirates' are, he knew they were hot on his tail."

"And he was worried," Suzanne said.

"Why is the railyard called 'Deception Gap'?" Detective Ryan asked. He hailed from east Texas.

"It sits between two hills," Tom explained, "both roughly the same height. But when you're standing on top of the hill to the west, it seems like you're at a higher elevation than the eastern hill."

"It's a trick of the landscape," Pete said. "The land between looks flat, but it slopes down a bit toward the east. The tops of the two hills are almost even."

"We've hiked them a hundred times," Kathy recalled with a smile.

Detective Ryan grunted. "Well, it's a suitable name for this caper. Someone is being deceptive, and there are some serious gaps in the story."

The Chief asked, "How did management handle Mr. Bradley's disappearance?"

"On the surface they're rankled because he didn't give notice," the investigator replied. "It seems good welders are hard to find. On the flip side, it was like no big deal. They said it happens all the time. People don't show and are never seen again."

"But he *did* show," Suzanne protested, replaying Heidi's words in her mind. "Not only that, but the railroad owed him for overtime and vacation pay."

"Don't forget his retirement account," Kathy reminded.

"Plus he left a bagged lunch in his car," Pete said.

"There's only one road in and out," Tom pointed out. "The security camera recorded him arriving at work—early, in fact. But he never left."

"Not alive, anyway," Pete said, with his typical dramatic flair.

Detective Ryan rubbed the back of his neck, a habit they'd seen before. "That's what makes this case so unique. The stationmaster tried selling me on the idea that Mr. Bradley must have jumped an outgoing train. I didn't buy it."

"You interviewed the management?" Kathy asked.

"Uh-huh," the detective replied. "And the workers too, which wasn't easy. The roundhouse runs twenty-four/seven in multiple shifts, so at the shift change lots of people are coming and going. To the best of my knowledge, we talked to every one of them."

"Nothing?" the Chief asked.

"No leads, that's for sure. A few workers spotted the young man. Two guys pulled up beside him in the parking lot, and one trailed Beau into the roundhouse. Another fellow witnessed him picking up some welding equipment, right at the shift change. After that . . . nothing."

There was a sharp knock at the door before it swung open. A uniformed officer ushered in Mrs. Anita Bradley, a tiny woman in her sixties with shocking white hair, wearing a stylish floral-print summer dress. She held an oversize purse close to her body. *Like a security blanket,* Suzanne thought. Everyone stood.

"Mrs. Bradley, I'm Detective Joe Ryan," he said, holding his hand out. "We talked on the telephone. Sorry to meet you under these circumstances."

"Thank you, sir." She grabbed his arm for a few seconds and searched his face. Her strong eastern accent rang out. Introductions followed before everyone sat down.

"Is there anything new on Beau?" she asked. "Anything at all?"

"No, not yet," Detective Ryan answered. "At least nothing that points to where your son is. However, these four young mystery searchers just came in with a rather startling development. Kathy, would you explain?"

"Mrs. Bradley, Beau sent us a text message an hour before he disappeared." Kathy pulled up the missive on her cell phone and handed it to the older woman.

"Would you read it to me, dear?" she asked. "My eyesight isn't as good as it used to be."

"Oh, sure." She read the message out loud.

"He said—'pirates,'" Mrs. Bradley said, her voice catching. "That's rather strange. What does it mean?"

"We don't know," Tom admitted, shaking his head.

"It's a mystery, ma'am," the detective said. "No clue yet what's going on at Deception Gap Railroad Yard. But we're working hard to solve this case and find your son."

"Dead—or alive?" she challenged, her voice catching again.

The Chief coughed once before replying. "Mrs. Bradley, at this stage we can only hope for the best. But so far there's no evidence of foul play."

"How long had Beau lived in Prescott?" Pete asked.

"Two years. Just before he graduated from welding school, he began searching for a job. He loved the Old West, and central Arizona seemed to have lots of it. So he answered an ad in your local newspaper—they hired him after one telephone interview."

"So it's obvious he enjoyed the work," Tom mused.

"Oh, yes," Mrs. Bradley said. "Until last month."

"What changed?" Suzanne asked.

In reply, she reached inside the cavernous purse resting on her lap and pulled out a letter. She handed it to Suzanne. "Here, read this, please—the yellow part."

The single-page letter—dated two weeks earlier and beginning with the salutation "Dear Mom"—had a yellow-highlighted paragraph toward the bottom. Suzanne read it out loud: "'Mom, I'm looking for another job in the Prescott area, or maybe farther north. Stuff's happening at Deception Gap that's troubling. Illegal stuff, I think. It's time I moved on. There's a job opening in Flagstaff, Arizona that looks promising.'"

Tears rolled down Mrs. Bradley's cheeks. She reached into her purse for a tissue and blew her nose. "I just pray that Beau is alive." She peered across the conference room table at the foursome. "My son seemed to have confidence in you. He came to you for help. Why?"

"We've been quite successful at solving mysteries," Pete explained. "We think he must have read about us in *The Daily Pilot*, our local newspaper, and sent that message."

"Well, that's interesting," she said. "Beau was always a huge newspaper reader—he wasn't ever into social media. Will you continue to search for him?"

The Chief and Detective Ryan exchanged glances.

"Mrs. Bradley," the Chief replied, "we've deployed all the

resources of Prescott City Police in the search for your son. That includes our homegrown mystery searchers here."

"Well, thank goodness," she said. "I am so appreciative. Beau was a good boy . . . never gave me a lick of trouble. Everyone liked him." She stopped and glanced around the room with conviction. "He would thank you if he were here, that's for sure."

"We'll do everything possible to find him," Kathy said, assuring her in a calm voice.

The poor woman appeared dead tired—her face spoke volumes. The sudden disappearance of her son and her worry for his welfare had taken a toll.

Suzanne asked, "Mrs. Bradley, where are you staying?"

"Across the street, at the Hassayampa Inn." The famous landmark had opened in 1927 and was a favorite of the Jacksons' and the Brunellis' parents, who often enjoyed dinner in the inn's Peacock Room.

"We'll stay in touch and advise you of our progress," Kathy said.

"Thank you, dear. I am more than grateful."

The uniformed officer appeared once more, and Mrs. Bradley soon retreated down the hallway.

Silence reigned for a few moments.

"Well, Detective Ryan, what's next?" Tom asked.

"Boss Zimmerman."

"Who's he?"

"He's the stationmaster at Deception Gap Railroad Yard. We'll set up a meeting for you. I'll tell him y'all are searching for Beau at his mother's request, which is true." He hesitated. It was easy to see his mind churning. "One thing. Don't mention that message you received from Beau Bradley."

Kathy said, "We won't say a word."

"Or who your father is," the Chief warned his twins. "It will help us all if he doesn't know about the access you have here. Don't give away anything you don't have to." He stared hard at the four over the rims of his glasses.

"He might have heard of them already," Detective Ryan said, glancing over at the Chief.

"That's a chance we'll have to take."

The mystery searchers nodded and chorused, "Got it."

"What kind of guy is he?" Pete asked.

Detective Ryan snorted. "Zimmerman? Difficult. Very. Don't expect a warm reception."

5

DECEPTION GAP

That, as things turned out, was a colossal understatement.

The mystery searchers had journeyed to Deception Gap Railroad Yard, north on Highway 89 through scenic boulder-strewn country. Natural canyon murals rippled past along both sides of the winding route. In the distance, not far either, northerly mountains poked up above the horizon and, to the west, the immense Prescott National Forest beckoned.

Pete was at the wheel of the Brunellis' Mustang.

"Next right on a gravel road," his sister said, pointing the way. "Then a quarter mile in."

"Got it." No problem finding a spot in the employee parking lot. It held about twenty cars—not even half full.

Tom glanced at the screen of his cell phone. Tuesday, 4:00 p.m. *Right on time,* he thought.

A small single-story building—white clapboard, not far from the railyard's parking lot and before the first set of tracks—boasted two offices. The front screen door led into a spacious reception area. Behind a large L-shaped desk sat an older lady with a pleasant manner who introduced herself as Shirley.

"I've been expecting you." She waved the mystery searchers into

Boss Zimmerman's dark, cave-like office. A sign on his credenza read MR. Z—his preferred nickname, as it turned out.

It wasn't long before things heated up.

Boss Zimmerman—a giant of a man, six foot five and two hundred and fifty pounds or more, Tom figured—glared across his desk at the foursome. His beefy face had turned a florid red; prodigious amounts of sweat poured off his forehead. There wasn't a shred of doubt that he resented their presence.

"Because he's crazy, that's why!" the stationmaster declared in a voice heavy with sarcasm, in response to Suzanne's insistent questions. "Why else would anyone leave us in a lurch like that?"

Standing off to one side was Mr. Zimmerman's assistant, Ben Wright—tall and trim, middle-aged, with a friendly face, dressed in jeans, a long-sleeved work shirt, and heavy boots. The mystery searchers couldn't help but like the man. "Call me Ben," he had said, smiling as they shook hands minutes earlier. Ben was working to keep a lid on things.

"Look, we get it," he said. "You are friends of his mother, trying to find Beau Bradley. And believe me, we're very concerned too. It's hard to understand why Beau rode off into the sunset."

Inwardly, Suzanne had risen to a slow boil, but on the surface, she kept her famous temper under control . . . just. Mr. Z was infuriating her. His eyes bore into her, but she glared right back, her face burning, all but ignoring Ben. "That doesn't match Mr. Bradley's personality," she snapped at the stationmaster. "He worked here for two years. I'll bet he was an outstanding employee."

Mr. Z had cornered himself, which seemed to irritate him even more. He leaned forward, staring hard at his four visitors—Suzanne first—jabbing at each of them with his index finger. "Okay, I'm finished arguing with you. The fact is that Beau Bradley left his job without notice, which we didn't appreciate one bit. We don't know why he took off, nor where he went. What else can we do?"

"Find Beau," Suzanne shot back. "Or discover what happened to him. We're not giving up until we get answers. People don't just 'disappear.'"

The stationmaster raised both arms in frustration. "You do whatever you want," he growled. "Just stay out of my hair."

An awkward silence descended before Tom broke the strange interlude. "Can we tour the railroad yard?"

"Not by yourselves," Mr. Z muttered.

"I'm more than happy to escort you," Ben offered. He winked at the foursome. "Follow me."

Mr. Z waved them away without another word, clearly relieved to see their backs. Detective Ryan, they knew, had pressured the man for a same-day meeting, which he had agreed to with great reluctance.

After stepping outside, Ben turned to them and lowered his voice. "Boss is a decent guy. He's just angry—he liked Beau, and good welders are hard to find, especially on short notice. Let's head out this way."

Deception Gap Railroad Yard was a massive enterprise. "The yard encompasses four hundred acres," Ben explained, "and the railway has operated here for a century and a half. We handle rail traffic between Los Angeles and Chicago, all the way through to the East Coast, and south to Phoenix. That's tons of freight passing through Prescott almost every day."

"Where does it all originate?" Tom asked.

"Mostly from the South Los Angeles shipyard, "Ben replied. "Goods from China, South Korea, Hong Kong, Taiwan, Japan—all over East Asia."

"A hundred and fifty years, you said?" Kathy asked. The buildings' grimy exteriors looked as if they hadn't seen a cleaning in decades. She was careful not to brush against them as they ambled past.

Ben chuckled. "The buildings look a little dilapidated, don't they? They date from the mid-nineteenth century, right after the Union Army arrived to establish the new territorial capital in 1864. President Lincoln wanted to prevent the Arizona Territory from getting into the hands of the Confederate South. What's surprising is that inside these old structures you'll find modern tools that keep the trains running on time."

Tom asked, "How long have you worked here, Ben?"

"Three years," he replied.

Pete's eyebrows shot up. He had figured Ben for a lifer. "Where were you before this?"

"Eight years stationed in South Korea," he replied with a slight smile. "I was an Army quartermaster. Boss hired me as soon as I got out. I'm slated to take over his job next year." It was easy to see that the prospect excited him. He led them over to a four-story tower, rising from the ground on spindly legs.

"Is this where you control traffic?" Pete asked.

"Yup. Anything moving, either coming or going—it's all managed upstairs. Let's say hello to Fred."

They followed Ben up a tight spiral staircase and straight onto the tower's main deck. A short, bald man with jowls and a mustache stood in front of an oversize computer screen, peering through binoculars and the huge windows toward the north. In the background they could hear intermittent two-way radio traffic.

"Welcome, welcome!" the man exclaimed, turning to greet his visitors. He set the binoculars on the inside window ledge and extended his hand. "Who do we have here?"

Ben introduced the four mystery searchers, remembering each of their names. It turned out the tower operator had a warm, friendly disposition.

"They're friends of Beau Bradley's mother," Ben explained, "trying to figure out what happened to Beau."

Fred's face dropped, and his smile faded away. "Oh, my goodness, please tell his mother that Fred Wilson is sorry for her loss. It's a terrible thing. I hope Beau shows up somewhere, and soon too."

"Thank you, sir," Tom said.

"We will," Kathy said. He reminded her of Papa Bob, her grandfather.

"Call me Fred," he prompted them.

As they gazed through the deck's spacious windows—edged open to counter the summer heat—the group enjoyed a perfect 360-degree view of the railroad yard. Two rows of freight cars rested side by side below them, one pulled by a pair of locomotives, the other with a locomotive pushing at the rear. To the south, a third train crawled into the railyard in slow motion. Multiple sets of tracks extended to the horizon, all aligned along a north-south axis. Half a dozen workers wandered below them, tools in hand, while another climbed atop a boxcar. Soft radio traffic continued in the background.

"Is the tower manned day and night?" Tom asked.

"Sure is," Fred replied, "daily except for midnight until four a.m., when the traffic grinds to a halt."

"Is the yard lit up at night?" Pete asked.

"When we're working, yes, for sure," Ben replied. "We light up the entire area and turn night into day. That way the tower operator doesn't miss a thing. But at midnight, the lights dim down."

"But not off?"

"Correct. Enough to see your way safely across the yard from the roundhouse to the parking lot—the whole caboodle dims down to ten percent. The buildings may look old, but our outdoor lighting system is up to date, all dimmable LEDs, centrally controlled, right here. During those hours, all work takes place in the roundhouse. Just a skeleton crew of welders and other guys, making essential repairs that just can't wait."

"On the day Beau vanished," Suzanne asked, "no one noticed anything unusual?"

Fred shook his head. "I didn't. My schedule calls for four days a week, ten-hour shifts, and I transition with the other operator starting at two in the afternoon. In fact, when Beau came to work that day, I watched him pull into the parking lot."

"Look over there." He pointed out a window and across the railyard. "You can see the front entrance of the roundhouse, plain as day." He paused his narrative for a few seconds. "That's where I last saw Beau, heading in to start his shift. It's a real shame. I got along well with him."

"You never saw him leave the roundhouse?" Kathy asked.

"Never. Hang on for a sec." He grabbed the binoculars and checked a line of freight cars before picking up a hand-held two-way radio: "Four-four-two, you're clear. Have a wonderful day." His finger jabbed toward the northbound freight train drawn by two locomotives. "That one is heading to Cheyenne, Wyoming."

"How many people work here?" Tom asked.

Fred looked to Ben for an answer.

"Close to forty."

"The day Beau disappeared," Suzanne asked, "he had the three o'clock shift?"

"Yes, he did," Fred replied, rubbing his chin. "But he always showed up fifteen or twenty minutes before the hour. A reliable guy —you could set your clock by him."

"Were there trains pulling out?" Tom quizzed.

"That day? Oh, sure, you bet. Two regular departures, the first one headed north to Cheyenne and the second south to Phoenix, both around four p.m."

"He couldn't have hidden inside a boxcar?" Pete asked.

"Oh, goodness no," Ben declared. He held one hand up for emphasis. "There's no way—none—that he could cross the yard and walk over to those trains without me seeing him. Not only that, but they seal those boxcars in L.A.—and they remain that way until their final destination."

They chatted for a few minutes more until Ben and his guests said their goodbyes, thanking Fred for his help. Tom wrote his cell phone number on a slip of paper and handed it to Fred. "If you think of anything else, please call us."

"You can count on me."

The mystery searchers followed Ben, descending the steep stairs back to ground level. In their minds, Fred's conviction that Beau Bradley could never have left the yard seemed to offer proof positive. Beau's remains *had* to be buried somewhere on the premises.

Pete decided to push a little further, asking Ben bluntly, "What do you think happened to Beau?"

"Well, Fred seems darn sure of himself. But Mr. Z thinks Beau might have driven one of the motorized people movers up the line and hidden himself on an outgoing train. We found one vehicle parked near the outer edge of the yard. That happens often, and no one pays the slightest attention to them . . . including Fred."

As they continued their tour, Ben called out the usage of each structure. "That's a chemical room for rust removal." He pointed to a squat one-story, plugging his nose as they passed by. "Stinks to high heaven." No one disagreed. "And this next one is where we store rarely used equipment."

Tom noticed some buildings with chained doors. He stopped beside the last one. "You don't use this as a workshop?"

"That's correct. Four of the older buildings haven't seen service for years, but things change. Once in a long while we'll find a use for the space. Then, just like that, its back in service."

The roundhouse loomed ahead. Two sets of tracks led in and out of the giant structure. The group strolled through its wide-open front doors. "One hundred feet wide," Ben stated. "This structure is our pride and joy, the place where we fuel and service the giant locomotives."

Suzanne trailed the group, taking in the immensity before her. Just before crossing in, she pivoted around and glanced back toward the tower. Fred Wilson stood high on the deck, arms folded, looking down at her through the spacious windows. She waved. Fred waved back.

6

THE ROUNDHOUSE

Deception Gap Railroad Yard was aptly named for more than one reason: the inside of the roundhouse appeared larger than the outside. It seemed to Tom that it covered two-thirds of a football field.

The structure's giant turntable was entirely indoors, which accounted for the building's mammoth size. As Ben explained, the turntable—capable of executing a slow 180—enabled a newly fueled or repaired locomotive to exit the building in a forward or backward motion, ready to push or pull a lengthy line of boxcars. "That's why it's called a roundhouse," Ben explained.

They headed toward a yellow glow emanating from giant portable lights on tall stands scattered around the floor. After passing a three-story-high crane stretching up into the shadowy rafters above, they strolled past half a dozen room-for-two motorized people movers—which reminded Tom of oversized golf carts—before arriving at a pair of brightly illuminated locomotives.

Bright as daylight, Pete thought, noting how the light faded into shadow around the periphery of the vast space.

A dozen men crawled over the two locomotives, their activity generating an incredible amount of noise. Sparks flew, and close up the hammering was deafening. A potent smell of hot metal permeated the air, leaving a horrible taste in everyone's mouth.

"Is this what Beau did?" Pete yelled into Ben's ear.

"Yes!" Ben shouted back. "Beau was an expert welder, one of the best. He worked here in the roundhouse and outside on the boxcars. Welding is vital to keep things running—which explains Boss's anger."

"You've replaced him?" Tom called out.

"Oh, for sure. As soon as we could. We had to. If we're short a welder, work slows down."

The group ambled over to the closest locomotive. Ben waved to three men working on "The beast," as he called it. They set their tools down and walked over to the visitors. The noise level dropped a few decibels. Ben introduced the foreman, Hank Rogers, a muscular guy wearing a work jacket and a curious expression.

"Pleased to meet ya," the man intoned. "I'd shake hands with ya, but as you can see, we're all covered in grease. Say hello to Billy Booker and Jack Riley."

"These guys keep the trains running," Ben said with more than a hint of pride. The three men seemed friendly enough. There was a little small talk before Ben mentioned the reason for their visit. "They're friends of Beau Bradley's mom."

The three men stiffened—not blatantly, Suzanne thought, but noticeably. The trio shook their heads in sympathy but said little. A minute later, Riley, the youngest member of the team, turned away without so much as a "bye." He crawled back under the locomotive and started hammering.

Soon enough, the mystery searchers said their goodbyes, but first Tom wanted to let the assistant stationmaster know what to expect. "Ben, we'll be staying on the search until we find out what happened to Beau."

"I get it," he replied. "Detective Ryan made that clear. If there's anything I can do . . ."

ON WEDNESDAY MORNING, AS THE FOUR YOUNG SLEUTHS WERE sitting in the large conference room at police headquarters and awaiting Detective Ryan, Boss Zimmerman's name came up often. There was talk about Hank Rogers and Billy Booker too—their reaction to Beau's name evoked a high level of interest. And then there was Jack Riley.

Kathy defended the young man. "Maybe he was behind on his work."

"You gotta be kidding," Pete said, screwing up his face in mock surprise. "We shocked that guy. He didn't expect to see anyone wandering around, asking questions."

"Ben mentioned Beau's name and they all reacted," Suzanne said. She agreed with Pete—something was off. *Way* off.

Pete felt vindicated. "You got that right."

Tom replayed the day's events in his mind. "Yeah, somehow, we surprised them—they didn't expect that."

"Expect *what?*" Pete demanded.

"That friends of Beau's family would show up," Tom replied, "asking questions. It made them nervous."

The Chief and Detective Ryan walked in and pulled up a couple chairs. "Okay," the detective said. "Fill us in."

"Well," Tom said, "it's just what you figured. Fred Wilson provided proof positive that Beau Bradley never left Deception Gap alive."

Detective Ryan concurred with that assessment. "Yup. When I interviewed Mr. Wilson, he told me he had never laid eyes on Beau again after he arrived for work on his last day."

"So he didn't hop on a freight train, nor did he make it back to his car," Suzanne said recalling their conversation with Heidi. "There were two trains leaving around the time Beau was at work—he didn't jump aboard either of them."

"Which means he's deader than a doornail," Pete deduced.

"We don't know that," his sister said.

"We don't know otherwise."

The Chief took a deep breath. "No matter what, it doesn't look good for the young man, does it?"

33

No one replied.

Jack Riley's actions triggered responses from everyone in the meeting. "That guy acted strange," Kathy said. "He knows something."

"Did you question him?" the Chief asked Detective Ryan.

"Sure. He told us he hadn't seen Beau that day."

"Can you run a background check on Riley?" Tom asked. "See if he has any criminal history?"

The detective grunted and wrote something in his notebook. "I've checked out Boss Zimmerman and Ben Wright. They're both clean as a whistle."

Suzanne asked, "What about Hank Rogers and Billy Booker?"

"And Fred Wilson," Kathy suggested. "Just in case."

"Uh-huh," the detective replied, jotting down the names.

The Chief leaned closer toward his homegrown mystery searchers. "It sounds like Boss Zimmerman didn't appreciate your visit."

"That's a fact," Suzanne said. "That guy is mean, and rude too. At one point, I thought he might spit at me."

That comment forced an involuntary chortle from Detective Ryan. "I warned you."

"His biggest beef," Pete said, "is that he thinks Beau took off without notice. That's a no-no in his book."

"Well," the Chief mused, "I'd feel the same way if one of my employees did that. Any boss would. Anything else there that looked suspicious?"

"No, other than that we triggered people just by showing up," Kathy declared.

Meanwhile, Tom's mind had wandered in a different direction. "I can't help wondering about the language Beau used in his text message."

"Meaning . . . ?" Detective Ryan asked.

"'Pirates,'" Suzanne said.

"Yup," Tom said. "It's such an interesting choice of word. What do pirates do?"

"Plunder," Kathy replied.

"Expensive stuff," Pete said, rubbing his hands together.

"So, in a railyard, that would have to be freight," Tom said. "From China and other countries in East Asia. There's nothing else worth plundering out there."

"We get that," the Chief said. "But when a freight train reaches the end of the line, people would notice any shortages. To the best of my knowledge, we've never seen a missing freight report from this railyard." He shot a questioning look to Detective Ryan. "Right, Joe?"

"That's right, Chief. I checked with the railroad. The last reported theft was three months ago, from a local shipment to Cheyenne." He shrugged. "They caught the guy."

"Well, it's an enigma," Tom said. He loved that word.

"Pirates plunder," Pete stated with conviction. "That's the bottom line. Beau must have meant something beyond ordinary theft."

Detective Ryan's eyes ticked over to Pete. "What you're saying is, Beau Bradley's disappearance must intersect with unreported criminal activities at Deception Gap. He's not around to tell us about them, so it's up to us to figure stuff out." He tossed out a challenge. "Right?"

"We'll do our best, sir," Tom replied. "What's the next move for Prescott City Police?"

Detective Ryan and the Chief exchanged looks. The Chief nodded.

"We've already made it," Ryan said. "Deception Gap has been hiring people." He paused again. "In fact, they just hired someone we're quite familiar with. The new employee's start date is tomorrow."

The mystery searchers glanced at one another, mystified.

"We don't get it," Kathy said. "I mean . . . they hired someone? Why—what does that have to do with the case?"

"This might turn into a murder investigation," Detective Ryan replied. His expression rarely changed, even when the topic was a possible murder, and right now was no exception. "And we don't

35

have any promising leads. Deception Gap's management doesn't realize it, but they've just hired one of Prescott's finest." He sat back with a self-satisfied smile.

"You mean an undercover officer?" Tom asked. Clearly, he liked the sound of that.

"Uh-huh. And don't ask for a name," the Chief counseled, his eyes searching the young faces around him. "God forbid if something went wrong out there. You're better off not knowing."

"But that person will know about *you*," Detective Ryan finished.

7

BLACKOUT

"**F**igure it out," Pete said, echoing Detective Ryan's words from earlier that day. "That's a tall order."

"Quit whining," his sister said, just to needle him.

"Okay. *You* figure it out."

The mystery searchers had met that evening at the Brunellis' house and were now sprawling around the family room. A strategic meeting was on the agenda. The Brunelli parents, Joe and Maria, wandered in and out.

"Lemonade, anyone?" Maria asked. It was a warm summer evening, and there was nothing like her homemade Italian-style lemonade. In fact, Maria's reputation as an outstanding Italian cook had withstood the test of time. For as long as the twins could remember, the Jacksons had been frequent guests for dinner at the Brunellis'—always a festive, *delicious* occasion.

A chorus of yeses and thank-yous rang out.

Tom started. "What are the goals?"

"Simple," Kathy said. "Detective Ryan challenged us to identify any criminal activity at the railroad yard. And Heidi wants us to find Beau—or his body."

"Oh, is that all?" Pete asked mockingly.

"There's a lot of pressure on Detective Ryan to find Beau—alive," Suzanne declared. "And we shouldn't jump to the conclusion that he's dead. That would be poor detective work. He may be hiding, or he may be *hidden*. We'll be competing with that undercover guy, whoever he is."

Pete flopped out on a sofa and stretched out his five-foot-ten frame, two inches shorter than his best friend's. "I dunno about 'simple,' but whatever's taking place out there must occur in the dead of the night. Otherwise, everyone would be on to it."

"That's interesting," Kathy said. "There are people working out there twenty-four/seven. Many of them must have no clue what's happening."

"Well, *duh*," her brother said. "What would you expect with forty people working in the roundhouse?"

"Just saying."

"Take Ben Wright and Fred Wilson, for example," Suzanne said. "I'll bet neither one is involved in criminal activity of any kind."

Tom asked, "What about Mr. Z?"

"If he's involved, he's in charge," Suzanne said, recalling the stationmaster's rudeness. Just the thought of Boss Zimmerman irked her. "He might be in this up to his oversize ears."

"Or perhaps he's just an angry man," Kathy said.

"Or the ringleader," Pete said.

"Could be none of the above," Suzanne added.

"And then there's Jack Riley," Tom put in.

"He's either in it, or he knows something," Suzanne mused. "Riley's behavior was odd, to say the least. Those background checks might pull up something."

"Well, whatever's going on," Pete surmised, "it happens when the traffic tower shuts down and they turn those lights down."

"Let's check things out," Tom said. "Tonight."

Kathy groaned. "Oh, brother. I hate those all-nighters."

Pete shot her a sly grin. "'Quit whining.'"

LATE WEDNESDAY EVENING, HALF AN HOUR BEFORE MIDNIGHT, KATHY parked the Brunellis' Mustang on a lonely dirt road. The mystery searchers had arrived on the eastern side of Deception Gap, on the far side of the bordering hill. An easy fifteen-minute hike along a well-worn path zigzagged its way to the top. It was a familiar climb —growing up as children in Prescott, they had often hiked the area. *But never in the middle of the night,* Suzanne thought.

"It's spooky," Kathy called out, giggling, halfway up. The only other sound was a million deafening cicadas.

A gentle breeze cooled the warm summer night. As they hiked closer to the summit, the sky grew considerably lighter. The darkness lifted the second they crested the hill to a view that took their breath away.

"*Dang,*" Pete exclaimed. "Check it out." Below them, the four hundred acres of Deception Gap were lit up like daylight.

There was movement in the tower—"That would be Fred," Suzanne noted—but the railyard was devoid of workers. Three lengthy lines of boxcars, a locomotive attached to each line, sat stationary.

"What stinks?" Pete asked, screwing up his face.

Suzanne replied, "It's that horrible metal smell. Imagine that— it's strong enough to reach up here."

"Not good."

From their vantage point, the foursome had a straight-line view of the expansive, open front doors of the roundhouse, with light oozing out from somewhere deep in the interior. It was business as usual: the intermittent sound of steel on steel penetrated the stillness.

"I bet those doors rarely close," Tom mused out loud, "no matter the time of year."

They broke out two pairs of binoculars and passed them back and forth, but there wasn't much to see. All the work seemed to be taking place inside the roundhouse.

At midnight they watched as Fred hit a switch and hundreds of powerful LED lights, some elevated high up on poles, others attached to the exterior walls of the buildings, began a sixty-second fade to ten percent. Another minute passed before the foursome's eyes adjusted, aided by the moonlit night.

"Fred's done," Kathy said.

"Yup," Pete said, "I can see him heading out to the parking lot." He stared through the binoculars, adjusting the focus ever so slightly.

"Yeah, I see him," Suzanne said, peering through the other set. "He's the only guy moving around . . . anywhere." Soon, Fred's head-lights cut into the night before he cranked left, his rear taillights quickly fading in the distance.

The foursome wandered the ridgeline in a vain attempt for better views of *something*. But there was no action, no movement of any kind.

"Plus, we need to get closer," Pete suggested as he marched back and forth. "Much closer." He was the impetuous one, always ready for the next adventure.

"Sure," Tom agreed. "But let's run a drone out there first. We'll haul a bird up here and fly it around the yard."

"Splendid idea," Suzanne affirmed. "Safer too."

"I'm with you," Kathy said.

Pete complained. "They could be stripping a railcar right now."

His sister rolled her eyes in the dark. "Oh, sure—right. Even though there's not a soul in sight."

Time dragged along until 2:00 a.m., when a group of five men exited the roundhouse and stood out front, smoking ciga-rettes. Light seeping through the front doors displayed backlit, silhouetted figures impossible to recognize.

"We've got a long way to go," Suzanne said.

"Meaning?" Tom asked.

"Meaning we've only met a fraction of the guys who work in the yard. What if the perps are standing right in front of us? We wouldn't have a clue."

Pete had an idea. "Hey, how about rolling out the bug, that

listening device we discovered in the Yavapai Courthouse Museum? We could hide it around those front doors."

"Not a chance," Tom declared, staring hard through the binoculars. He circled the entire frame. "No place to hide it, even if we could pull off the installation without anyone noticing."

Minutes later, the five men strolled back into the mammoth structure.

Then nothing, except a little hammering from the roundhouse. The metal smell came and went with the breeze as the four huddled for the next hour, tossing ideas back and forth. The night turned cooler.

It was Pete who dreamed up another winning idea—one they all liked: lure the "pirates" into the open with bait planted in the local paper. They kicked the details around for half an hour before calling it quits at 3:00 a.m.

"Thank the Lord," Kathy grumbled with relief, heading home at long last.

ON THURSDAY, AFTER SLEEPING IN TO CATCH A LITTLE EXTRA shuteye, the mystery searchers trooped down to police headquarters to report on their midnight run.

"Nothing much to tell," Suzanne admitted. "Quiet as a mouse out there."

"Well, that's not too surprising, is it? You'd have to be lucky to catch them in the act." Detective Ryan hesitated a few seconds before adding, "Whatever that might be."

"It would help if we knew what we were looking for," Tom groused. Lack of sleep made him edgy.

"I feel for you," the detective said, eyeing him with a chuckle, "but that's police work for you." He was well aware of the twins' ambition to follow their father's footsteps into law enforcement. "It's often a wait-and-see game, and there are plenty of lonely vigils. Anyway, I've got something here for you."

He searched through papers bundled on the conference room table. "First, Jack Riley is clean: no wants, no warrants, not even a parking ticket. He graduated from Prescott High three years ago, then attended a two-year technical school in Phoenix. This is his first job."

"Wait a sec!" Kathy exclaimed. "That's *our* school. He was only four years ahead of us."

"I wonder if Heidi knew him," Suzanne wondered out loud. "She attended Prescott High back in the day."

"When did he start working at Deception Gap?" Pete asked.

The investigator rifled through his notes. "Two years ago. They hired him right out of industrial school—top of his class. The guy's a loner. According to his teachers, he didn't have much to do with anyone. But he's reliable and a hard worker—I doubt whether he'd be involved in any criminal activity."

"Well, he knows *something*," Suzanne said. "His behavior was weird, to say the least. How do we get him talking?"

"Engage him," Detective Ryan suggested. "People talk when you're friendly toward them. He might surprise you."

"Wouldn't it have more weight coming from you?" Tom asked.

"Yeah, could be," the officer replied, pursing his lips. "But 'weight' might not be what you want. I think you should do the asking. Questions from a police detective might put him on the defensive. In fact, if Heidi knows him, that could make all the difference."

"We'll call her," Kathy said.

The investigator picked up the thread. "Fred Wilson is clean too. Nothing negative in his background—he's a family guy." He paused a few seconds, shuffling through paper. "Different story for Hank Rogers and Billy Booker."

"Tell us," Pete said, his eyes gleaming with anticipation.

"They go back a long way. Both have criminal records—small stuff, beginning with shoplifting. They hawked stolen merchandise online, which was easy to trace. We caught 'em. In their early twenties, they graduated to grand theft auto—stealing cars and running them to Mexico. They got nailed crossing the border in a stolen Mercedes and served time together at Arizona State Prison in Florence." He paused. "Nothing since."

"Hmm," said Tom. "With records like that, they're lucky that Mr. Z hired them."

Kathy said, "It's possible that they've graduated into more serious crime."

Pete's eyebrows shot up. "Like bumping somebody off?" he asked.

"One thing for sure," Tom said, "they've got sticky fingers. Maybe it's a bad habit."

"Well . . ." Suzanne began. She had bided her time, waiting for the right moment. "We've got something a little sticky too."

Detective Ryan turned to her, looking puzzled. *"Sticky?"*

"Yeah, well sorta. We came up with an idea . . . a false-flag strategy."

Pete cut to the chase. It had been his idea, after all. "Look," he said, winding up to make his case. "Either Beau is dead and buried somewhere in Deception Gap, or he departed for parts unknown. We all agree he didn't cut out of Dodge, so his body's *gotta* be buried somewhere in or near the railyard. Right?"

The detective leaned back and stretched his arms high behind him. "There's no proof the young man died."

"That's true," Tom said. "But if we plant a false-flag story in *The Daily Pilot*, we might flush these 'pirates,' as Beau called them, out into the open. Maybe they'll meet up, or—"

"Or lead us to the body," Pete jumped back in. He held his hands up as everyone glanced his way. "Just saying. It's possible . . . anything's possible."

Nothing ever seemed to excite the seasoned officer, but it was obvious he liked the idea. "So the story is, what? That we picked up some information on the case?"

"Exactly," Pete said. He stood up, brimming with enthusiasm. "That someone squealed, or a rumor came in. Something with meat on it."

"Then we'll track the three most interesting guys when they get off work," Kathy explained. "See where they go, what they do."

"And whether they meet up or not," Suzanne added.

"Which three?" the detective asked.

"Hank Rogers, Billy Booker, and Jack Riley," Pete replied. He sat back down.

"Don't forget about Boss Zimmerman," Tom said, tossing in the big man's name. "And we'll need a watcher on the east hill, tracking the subjects as they leave the parking lot." *Tracking* was police terminology that Tom particularly liked.

Detective Ryan chuckled. "I'll handle Zimmerman. Should be interesting. Who's gonna call Heidi?"

8

THE PLAN UNFOLDS

H eidi returned Suzanne's call minutes later. The mystery searchers briefed her on the events of the last couple of days, leading up to their request for a false-flag story. But no one mentioned the word *false-flag*.

"Here's the reason for the call, Heidi," Suzanne said, reeling their favorite reporter deeper into the mystery. "In a few minutes, you'll receive a call from Detective Ryan inviting you to a news conference this afternoon. There's a lead coming in on the Deception Gap story, a major break. It's important that the information he receives jumps onto the front page tomorrow morning."

"Wait a sec," Heidi protested. "You're telling me about a lead that *hasn't* come in yet . . . but *will* come in today?"

"Exacto," Pete replied.

"What kind of a lead are we talking about?" she asked guardedly.

"A source has information about what happened at Deception Gap," Tom replied. "But we can't disclose anything else."

"Oh. I get it," Heidi said flatly. She knew—they *all* knew—that a reporter can't knowingly run a false story, nor can a newspaper print one. "Okay. If it helps find Beau, I'll play ball. Hopefully, my editor will too."

Kathy couldn't wait to ask. "Heidi, did you go to high school with a guy named Jack Riley?"

"Did I ever," she replied. "That little turnip owes me. I had to defend him more than once."

"Did you get along well with him?"

"Jack? Oh, sure. He's the opposite of me. Quiet and shy—I did all the talking. That's why we got along so well. Why are you asking?"

"He works out at Deception Gap, and we think he knows something," Pete explained. "Detective Ryan wants us to engage him."

"Count me in," Heidi said with a laugh. "I'll shock the heck out of him. He's not your mysterious informant, is he?"

"Not yet," Kathy replied, stifling a giggle.

Next, the foursome prevailed upon their parents. In addition to the Brunellis' Mustang and the Jacksons' Chevy Impala, they required two additional cars: they'd need to follow three suspects, which required the same number of vehicles—plus one more for Suzanne, who volunteered to be the watcher. Detective Ryan would provide his own vehicle to tail Boss Zimmerman.

All four parents bought into the plan, although Sherri agreed with a healthy dose of apprehension.

"I'll take Jack Riley," Pete announced.

"Who put you in charge?" his sister challenged.

"Me."

They also required a better communications system. Tom used WhatsApp to set up a group chat on their cell phones and included Detective Ryan in the loop. When it came to technology outside the boundaries of criminal activity, their favorite investigator was the least technical person they knew.

"Cool," he said. An astonished look had crossed his face as Tom showed him how the single-click login worked. "Never seen this before. It's better than my two-way radio."

"Two-way radios are a relic from the past," Pete said, sounding very sure of himself. "This technology uses Wi-Fi or satellite transmission with global coverage." That little diatribe didn't sit well with Detective Ryan, earning Pete a certain *look*.

46

"Your technology lesson didn't go over to well," Kathy quipped, giggling, as soon as the detective was out of earshot.

"What about Beau's mom?" Suzanne asked. "We need to clue her in before she reads the story in the *Pilot*."

AFTER DINNER, THE MYSTERY SEARCHERS TROOPED OVER TO THE Hassayampa Inn and met Mrs. Bradley in the hotel's elegant dining room. The Peacock Room had emptied, providing enough privacy to gather in one of the comfortable horseshoe-shaped booths. Beau's mother—always fashionably dressed, the girls noted—sat between the four of them.

"Oh, goodness," Mrs. Bradley said. Her voice shook and her eyes watered more than once. "The police agreed to this . . . what did you call it? A false flag?"

"Certainly did," Suzanne assured the older woman. "They liked the idea too. We're all hoping it pushes the pirates into action."

"Meantime, we'll track the movements of possible suspects," Tom said. "Tomorrow afternoon, right after the shift change."

Tea arrived. Mrs. Bradley added in copious amounts of cream and sugar, much to Kathy's dismay. Kathy had cut sugar from her diet recently. She had to admit to herself that Mrs. Bradley's tea sure looked tasty.

"Has there been any indication where Beau might have gone?" Mrs. Bradley asked.

"Nothing yet," Suzanne admitted. "But this could point us in the right direction."

"What are you expecting?" Mrs. Bradley asked. "Your false-flag story won't say much." A tissue appeared from nowhere as she wiped her eyes. She blew on the hot tea before taking a sip.

No one wanted to talk about the possibility of a body.

Tom explained, "All we're looking for is guilty conduct. That should tell us if we're on the right track—or not."

Kathy grinned. "Is that a play on words?"

A COPY OF *THE DAILY PILOT* SLAMMED ONTO THE JACKSONS' DRIVEWAY before skidding to a stop. Tom raced out and flipped the newspaper to the front page. *There.* The headline on a small boxed bulletin toward the bottom read, "Police report tip on missing person."

He turned back into the house, shouting, "*Suzie!* Check it out!"

His sister bolted down the stairs and joined their parents at the kitchen table. Tom spread the paper across the table—right over his father's coffee cup—and read the story out loud. "An anonymous call came into the Prescott City Police tip line yesterday. In a late afternoon news conference, Detective Joe Ryan revealed that a caller had left a voice message claiming insider knowledge pertinent to a missing-persons case. Beau Bradley, a welder at Deception Gap Railroad Yard, disappeared last Sunday evening under suspicious circumstances. The caller asked for a 'no charges' guarantee in exchange for information regarding Mr. Bradley and stated that a follow-up call would occur shortly. With the investigation still in its infancy, Detective Ryan refused to answer questions."

Suzanne giggled as she glanced at her brother. "How does it feel to cause so much trouble, Mr. Anonymous?"

The Chief chortled. He retrieved his coffee cup from beneath the newspaper. "It'll be interesting to see what bubbles to the surface."

"Nice, huh?" Tom replied. He flashed an ear-to-ear grin. The four mystery searchers had scripted the message, and Tom had made the call—to Detective Ryan—from police headquarters. "Pete had a brilliant idea. Now let's see if his false flag works."

Suzanne couldn't hide her amusement as she nudged her brother. "It's always better to tell the truth."

The twins' mother, Sherri—a social worker for Yavapai County —wasn't having any of it. "I don't like the sound of this. These guys are dangerous."

"Oh, Mom," Suzanne replied, slipping an arm around her. The cautious nature of the twins' mother was legendary. "We're very careful, aren't we, Tom? Nothing will happen to us."

"Joe Ryan is running the case," her husband assured his wife. "Should be fine." He loved the idea that his twins wanted to follow him into police work.

Sherri's face spoke volumes. "Where have I heard that before?"

———

SUZANNE SUMMITED THE EAST HILL, HIGH ABOVE DECEPTION GAP, ON Friday in the mid-afternoon, just ahead of the shift change. She wore a floppy hat to deflect the blazing summer sun. Soon—after retrieving a set of binoculars and her cell phone from her backpack —she lay sprawled across the highest point of the ridgeline, training her eyes on the familiar view below.

"Hi, Fred," she murmured to herself. He sat in the control tower, perched on his high pivoting chair—a tiny, faraway figure—arms folded, looking across the railyard to the north. Two workers ambled toward the roundhouse, reminding Suzanne of moving toys on a child's train set. In the distance, heading south, she watched a locomotive and dozens of boxcars slowly making their way into the yard. Meanwhile, a steady stream of cars drove into the parking lot. *The next shift.*

Minutes later, about twenty men in work clothes—many carrying lunchboxes—plodded their way toward the parking lot. She zeroed in on Hank Rogers and Billy Booker, walking together and deep in conversation. A third man joined them: another heavy-set guy wearing overalls. Suzanne adjusted the binoculars and focused on the stranger. "Who are you?" she whispered to herself.

Booker was the first to reach his vehicle, but three cars preceded him out of the lot.

Suzanne reached for her cell and tapped the WhatsApp icon. "Kathy, Billy Booker on the way, car number four out of the lot."

Kathy's voice came right back. "Got it."

Seconds later, Hank Rogers drove off, just two cars behind Booker. Suzanne touched the open app: "Tom, your guy is in car number six."

"I'm on it."

Suzanne kept track of the departing cars, noting each one by tracing in the dirt with her finger and crossing off groups of five.

"Where's Mr. Riley?" Pete demanded.

"Hang on," Suzanne replied. *Patience.* "He's just walking across the last set of tracks." The man lagged back, waiting. When his fellow workers were all on their way, Riley spurted forward and jumped into his front seat. "He's on the way, Pete. Vehicle number eighteen—a small beige pickup."

"He's mine," Pete's voice burst back with gusto. He couldn't wait.

Then, silence. Suzanne knew that Detective Ryan sat in his car, waiting a few blocks from the intersection where the access road leading to Deception Gap met the highway that connected to the city. Unlike Pete, the detective was a patient man. Not a word from him as he waited for Boss Zimmerman.

Fifteen minutes later, Kathy reported in. "Looks like my guy is home. He walked into a street-side apartment on Fourteenth Avenue carrying his lunchbox. I'll park here with a view of his door."

Pete was next, his voice strangely muffled. "Jack is home. I've got a terrific view of his apartment." Kathy grinned—she figured her brother was chomping on a humongous apple he had snagged from the fridge. All four mystery searchers had brought food. No matter what, it promised to be a long evening.

A minute later, Tom called in. "I think Roger knows he's being tailed. He seems to be driving evasively, like he's trying to lose me. I'm breaking off following him."

More silence. An hour crawled past before an exasperated Suzanne touched her screen. "Detective Ryan, do you think he's *ever* coming out?"

There was a slight pause. "Yup. He'll be heading home soon." It was close to six o'clock. In the background, Suzanne heard the baseball game playing from his car radio.

"Who's winning?" she asked.

"The Diamondbacks, four-to-one."

"Hooray."

Pete couldn't resist. "About time."

Ten minutes later, Suzanne spotted the obnoxious Mr. Z lumbering along on his way to the employee parking lot. *Like a bear,* she thought. "He's on the way."

"Got it, thanks."

Suzanne, lying flat along the ridgeline for so long, stood and stretched. The sun had just set below the mountains to the west. She pulled off her floppy hat, ran her fingers through her long auburn hair, and twisted her stiff neck in a circle. She fell to one knee and retrieved her cell phone and binoculars, stuffing them into her backpack. Then, just before turning to walk down the hill, she glanced back for a last look into Deception Gap Railroad Yard.

In the fading light, she noticed the yard's lights were already glowing. Two freight trains were on the move, crawling along the snake-like rails—one arriving, the other departing. Workers criss-crossed the yard in no real hurry, slipping in and out of the round-house on their way to individual assignments. It was just another normal day. Or was it?

In the distance, she glanced over to the control tower, surprised —*shocked*—to see Fred Wilson, standing straight up, binoculars glued to his face, looking in her direction. *What the heck?* She reached into her backpack and retrieved the binoculars, raising them to focus on the tower windows.

There was Fred, all right. And not just staring in her direction— staring right at her. So intensely, in fact, that for a few seconds they locked eyes.

Suzanne groaned out loud, knowing it was too late. *Busted.* She gave him a little wave. He waved back.

9

ACTION ITEMS

On Saturday morning, the mystery searchers caught up with Detective Ryan at their favorite meeting spot. The Shake Shack was a discovery from their junior high years.

"What's not to like?" Pete had said back then. "Big, fat burgers and delicious, thick shakes. I mean, *come on!*" The boys ordered two shakes—chocolate and vanilla.

The girls had graduated to coffee in the morning and ordered an extra one for Detective Ryan. He arrived minutes later.

"Sorry." He found a seat between Tom and Pete, across from Suzanne and Kathy. "Crazy day for me. Have they improved the coffee here?"

"Uh-huh," Kathy replied. "It's—it's drinkable."

"Drinkable?" He sipped the still hot coffee and grimaced. "The stuff at the station is better, and that's saying something. Pass the cream. What's on the schedule?"

"Well," Suzanne began, "everyone drove home and stayed there...except Billy Booker."

The detective glanced over. "What happened to him?"

"He zipped over to his local Safeway and picked up a few

groceries," Kathy replied, "just before dinner. I followed him both ways. Lights out at eleven, and I headed home."

"I tracked Jack Riley," Pete said. "The guy went to his apartment, turned on his computer monitor, and never left the house. Just my luck, he didn't hit the sack until midnight."

The detective nodded. "Police work can be like that."

As in, long and boring, Pete thought. He enjoyed the adventure but had no desire to pursue a career in law enforcement. His thing was engineering. "What about Boss Zimmerman?"

"Drove straight home," the investigator said. "Lives by himself, never moved the entire evening. Lights out at ten-ish."

"That leaves Hank Rogers," Tom said. "The guy started zigzagging on his way into the city." He raised one hand and twisted it around in the air to show Rogers's evasive action. "It was obvious he was checking for a tail. I dropped out fast."

"Excellent move," Detective Ryan said. He sipped his coffee again, squeezing his eyes shut for a second or two.

"People with nothing to hide don't take evasive action," Tom said.

"So his actions suggest there's a good chance he's one of the pirates," Pete said.

"In which case," the detective added, "the exercise was well worth the trouble. Now we've confirmed our first serious lead."

"One step in the right direction," Kathy said.

"We might have to track Rogers in the future," Pete said. "Remember those GPS bugs we used at the Yavapai Courthouse Museum . . . the ones we hid in the artifacts? Well, we can borrow one from the school technology club again. I vote that we attach it to Hank Rogers's car."

"I second that," Tom said.

"Me too," Suzanne said. "We can slip it under a rear wheel well. Then we'll follow the guy with that app on our cell phones."

"Let's grab the drone at the same time," Kathy suggested.

"For sure," Pete agreed. "We wanna see what's happening out there."

"Be careful," Detective Ryan warned. "These guys play hardball. Just ask Beau Bradley's mother."

It was a sobering thought.

Suzanne raised her hand sheepishly. "One thing. Yesterday, when I stood up to leave the hill overlooking Deception Gap, I looked back at the yard. Right away I noticed Fred Wilson standing in the control tower. He appeared to be looking in my general direction—through his binoculars. I wondered what the heck he was staring at, so I pulled out my binoculars and focused on him." She paused.

"Well, what *was* he staring at?" Kathy asked.

"Not what, who. *Me.*"

"Oh, man," said Pete. "We're busted."

"Maybe not," Tom said. "I'd bet Fred Wilson is on our side."

"The question is, who's on the other side?" Suzanne asked.

Silence.

"Do any of us consider Mr. Wilson a threat in any way?" Detective Ryan asked, his voice calm and professional as ever. Nothing seemed to faze him. His cool demeanor was an inspiration to all four of the young detectives.

The mystery searchers glanced at one another before Suzanne piped up again. "I don't. He sure liked Beau Bradley. There's no doubt in my mind that he's an asset."

There was a murmur of agreement.

"So we all agree," the detective said. "He impressed me as a straight shooter too—let's not worry about him." His cell phone buzzed. Seconds later, he disconnected, stood and tossed his coffee cup—almost full—into a garbage can. "Sorry, gotta run. Keep me in the loop." Within a minute, he was on his way back to the station.

Pete rubbed his hands together. "Okay. How're we gonna do this?"

Tom grinned. His best friend was always ready for action. "We need the hardware. I'll call Ray Huntley and ask his permission." Ray was the president of the school technology club.

"The equipment is at his house for the summer, remember?" Suzanne said. "As long as he's in town, shouldn't be a problem."

"Do we all still have the GPS tracker app up to date on our phones?" Kathy asked. The mystery searchers had downloaded the application to help them catch the criminals in their second adventure, the mystery of the ghost in the county courthouse. With three more successful cases under their belts since, it seemed like forever ago.

Tom, the technology guru, pulled out his cell phone. "Sure do. I've never deleted it. Here it is, and right up to date." He tapped the screen and held it toward them. "Even better than before. Check out the app's new graphics."

"All righty," Suzanne exclaimed. "We'll plan on rolling out the drone tomorrow."

"Sunday night at midnight," Pete agreed. *Yeah.*

Kathy bit her lip. No sense complaining. "Who'll attach the tracker to Hank Rogers's car?"

"Me, of course," Pete replied. "We'll pay another daytime visit to Deception Gap, pull into the parking lot, and deploy it as we walk in."

"When?"

"If we can grab the hardware, what's wrong with today?" Pete asked. "They'll be working—that place never closes."

"What happens if Mr. Wilson spots you?" Kathy challenged.

"You don't want to go there."

"What about Jack Riley?" Tom asked.

"What about him?"

"We can't all take him on."

"Why not?"

"Well, think about it," Suzanne offered. "Detective Ryan says he's a loner. If we all showed up on his doorstep, we'd freak him out. Kathy and I will partner up with Heidi."

"He's a morning-shift guy," Pete recalled. "He's off at three today."

"Okay," Kathy said, "We'll call Heidi and see if she can make it."

Tom's face lit up. "Great! Meanwhile, Pete and I will return to Deception Gap."

"What for?" Kathy quizzed.

"Heidi mentioned security camera discs . . . we need to check them out."

Pete high-fived him. "Good idea, bro. Let's do it."

An image of Zimmerman's face flashed through Suzanne's mind. "Lucky you."

A THREAT

Tom spun the wheel of the white Chevy, cranking the car onto the lonely access road. They had called ahead—even though it was a Saturday afternoon, Deception Gap ran full on twenty-four/seven—except for those four-hour midnight grey-outs. People were at work, just as on any weekday.

Including Mr. Z.

Pete rode in the front passenger seat, humming to some imaginary tune playing in his mind, grateful that Ray had come through with the hardware. "Hey, this should be easy. Detective Ryan already scanned the security video footage. No one's gonna complain if we ask to see it."

Tom had a different idea. "Remember what Heidi said? He scanned through the disc for the *day* Beau disappeared. We'll go back in time and check *every* disc they've saved. Who knows? We might get lucky and find a clue."

"Well, let's hope they archive that stuff for longer than a week or two."

Three minutes later, Tom pulled into the parking lot. "Ten to one Fred Wilson already spotted us." The boys peered up toward the tower, but the afternoon sun reflecting off the expansive windows blinded them.

"Yup," Pete replied. "Nothing gets past Fred. Do you think he has a clue about what happened to Beau?"

"Not really. He's a friendly-enough guy, though."

"True. And he sure seemed to like Beau."

"So he said. Which vehicle belongs to Rogers?"

Pete peered ahead. "Last one on the right, the older, dark-blue SUV. *Whoa.* Wait a sec. There's a space right beside his car." Pete's trademark grin appeared as he squeezed the GPS tracker gently in one hand. "How easy is that? There's no way Wilson can see anything—our car will shield us from his view."

Tom nosed in and parked while Pete eased the passenger door open and dropped to the ground. He slipped the tracker—which was just a little larger and about twice the thickness of a man's watch case—under the left rear wheel well of Rogers's vehicle. He felt around with his fingers. *Click!* The tracker's magnet attached itself securely to the vehicle's steel frame. Pete rejoined Tom, who was pretending to tie a shoelace in front of the Chevy. Together, the boys strolled across the yard, heading toward the stationmaster's office.

"Here we go," Tom murmured. The boys walked up to the now-familiar white clapboard building. They opened a screen door and stepped into the interior. Two women were working away at their computers. Shirley glanced up.

"Oh, hello," she said, greeting them with a smile. "Tom, Pete."

An observant person, Tom noted—she remembered the boys' names from their earlier visit. Friendly too.

Shirley folded her hands under her chin. "Welcome back. How can I help you?"

"We were wondering if we could talk to Mr. Zimmerman," Tom replied.

"Oh, I'm sorry. He and Fred Wilson are meeting in the control tower. He can't be disturbed right now."

"What about Ben Wright?" Pete asked.

"Let me call him for you," she replied. "Please, sit down and make yourselves comfortable." She picked up a microphone that hung on the wall beside her and pushed a red button. *"Ben Wright, you have visitors . . . Visitors for Ben Wright."*

Her voice boomed out from dozens of outdoor speakers, creating an echo that vibrated in the stationmaster's offices before fading away in the distance.

"Oh, wow," Pete said. "You must have speakers everywhere."

"All over the yard," Shirley replied, "and throughout the round-house too. He'll get the message no matter where he is. Have you met Olivia? She's my assistant."

The boys stood and introduced themselves, shaking hands with Olivia, a demure young woman with short brown hair and a ready smile. Pete figured she was only three or four years older than he and Tom were. They chatted.

Five minutes later, the screen door banged open as Ben Wright strode in. His face lit up in recognition. "Tom and Pete, right? Great to see you." He shook hands with the boys. "What brings you out here? Good news, I hope."

"Nothing yet," Pete replied. "Except Detective Ryan got a tip from an anonymous caller."

"Oh, sure, we read all about it in the *Pilot*," Mr. Wright said. "How did that pan out?"

"He hasn't heard from the guy again," Tom replied.

"Maybe it's a hoax," Mr. Wright suggested.

Shirley had been listening to every word, a deep frown on her face. "I *hope* not. It's a terrible thing that Beau just plain disappeared."

"Yes, it is," Mr. Wright said, nodding. He glanced back to the boys. "Now, how I can help you?"

"Well," Tom replied, "we were wondering how long you keep the recordings from the camera that covers the end of the access road and the parking lot."

Ben hesitated. "Geez, I dunno. A week, I'd guess."

"Nope, I've got a month's worth right here," Shirley said primly.

She pointed to a small stack of four-inch discs on the top of a credenza.

Woo-hoo! Pete yelped silently. They were in luck. "Any problem if we look through them?"

Shirley glanced over toward Ben.

He nodded, his head tilting in surprise. "Sure, go for it. But the police checked them out earlier. What the heck are you looking for?"

"We're not sure," Tom replied with a shrug. "Anything unusual about Beau." *And evidence of anything strange,* he thought. *Or deadly.*

Shirley handed the discs to Tom and pointed to an empty desk pushed against the entrance wall. An old monitor rested on top. "Use that computer if you'd like. Boot it up and Olivia will log in for you."

Ben dragged two old wooden chairs over. "I'll leave you to it. If you see anything worthwhile, give me a shout." The screen door banged once more as he hustled away.

Shirley shook her head and returned to work. "Why that man always has to let that door slam, I'll never know."

Soon, the boys hunkered around the screen, fast-forwarding through one disc after another, slipping back into play mode each time Beau appeared. The camera's position allowed a wide-angle view that took in most of the parking lot and the first few yards of the walkway leading toward the railyard.

So tedious and slow, thought Tom. *And such pixilated footage.* Why the railyard had never upgraded from this ancient fossil DVD-ROM system to a modern one that could upload footage in real time to the Cloud was just plain incomprehensible to him.

The boys plugged in the oldest disc—each had a week's worth of content—and worked forward. As the days slipped by on-screen, they noted that Beau seemed to have a habit of avoiding the other workers. Even if he arrived at the same time as some of the other guys, he walked to his job site by himself and rarely talked to anyone.

"Except for Jack Riley," Tom noted. Twice, the boys watched

Beau and Jack walking together, chatting as they headed toward the roundhouse—and once as they strolled back. Still, there wasn't a real clue anywhere . . .

Until the second-last day's footage.

Pete inserted the final disc and skipped ahead. Whenever Beau appeared, the boys would hit Play and view Beau's arrival, then almost always just fast-forward to his departure. The man seldom reappeared in between, except occasionally to fetch something innocuous from his car, such as his lunch.

"Two days left," Pete said. Was this a waste of time?

Tom advanced to a few minutes before 3:00 p.m. "Here he comes." The grainy footage—at least it was in color—displayed Beau parking his car and leaning over to his right in the front seat.

"Hiding his wallet in the glove box again . . ." Pete said. "A man of habit." Beau stepped out of the car; the boys watched as he glanced back and clicked his key fob. His taillights blinked twice.

"Whoa," Tom whispered. He glanced over at the two women. Both were busy handling incoming phone calls. *"Look at that."* Just as Beau reached Hank Rogers's vehicle, the doors of the parked dark-blue SUV opened.

Pete straightened up in his chair. *"Crap. I never even spotted them."*

"Me neither. That's Hank Rogers."

The burly man stepped from the vehicle as Billy Booker jumped out from the passenger side. Beau froze in his tracks. In an instant the two men were in his face—visibly angry, hands waving in the air, ripping into him. *"A warning,"* Tom whispered. And then Hank Rogers poked the young man in the chest for good measure—hard.

"Just in case he didn't get the message," Pete murmured.

Other cars pulled into the parking lot, forcing Rogers and Booker to turn and walk away. Beau hesitated for a few seconds before he continued on his way toward the roundhouse.

Tom looked at Pete. "The message being . . . ?"

"My guess? 'Keep your mouth shut, or else.'"

A STICKY CLUE

Meanwhile, Suzanne and Kathy swung over to *The Daily Pilot* and picked up Heidi. The diminutive reporter dived into the backseat, excited at the prospect of reconnecting with her old high school friend.

"Jack's a nice guy," she declared. "We hung around together for a year or two."

Minutes later, Kathy parked behind Jack's pickup and the three made their way to his apartment. He lived on the ground floor of a single-story building in which each suite had its own front door, like a small motel.

Kathy knocked. Seconds passed before a chain rattled on the other side of the door. But no one answered.

"Mr. Riley, it's Suzanne Jackson and Kathy Brunelli," Suzanne called out. "Remember us? We met you the other day at Deception Gap. We're hoping you might be able to help us."

No response.

Kathy knocked again, a trifle harder.

"Go away," a muffled voice called out.

"We'd just like to talk to you for a few minutes, please, sir," Kathy said.

"Better us than the police," Suzanne muttered under her breath.

That's when Heidi chimed in. "Jack, it's Heidi Hoover! Open this door and talk to us. Now!" People rarely argued with Heidi—it was pretty much a waste of time.

The chain rattled again. The girls heard a click before the door opened an inch. They could see Jack, one eye peering out at them. "Heidi." A faint smile appeared on his face. "Long time, no see."

"Open up!" she said, laughing out loud. "You haven't changed a bit, have you?"

A sheepish Jack Riley swung the door wider. "No, and you haven't either. Still as pushy as ever." Dressed in jeans and a white undershirt, he wore no socks or shoes. He stared at the three of them, one after another.

"C'mon, Jack, invite us in," Heidi said, obviously annoying the poor guy.

He glanced back inside his apartment. Then, "Yeah, yeah," he said before the door swung open.

The three walked into a bachelor pad's tiny kitchen, with a table, two chairs, and a low ceiling. The place stank of stale smoke—a smell that Kathy hated. Jack cleared some dirty breakfast dishes off the table but left a cup of coffee, a pack of cigarettes, and an ashtray. He found two folding chairs in a closet and set them up without saying a word.

Suzanne felt sorry for him. He made no eye contact and seemed nervous. *Out of his element*, she thought.

Heidi, an experienced interviewer, waited until Jack sat down before opening the conversation. "Jack, you know why we're here."

He replied in a calm voice, staring right back at her. "I do not."

"Sure you do."

"The heck I do."

"Beau Bradley is missing," Suzanne said in an even tone. "His mother is here, in the city, waiting for him to turn up—dead or alive. You know something—whatever that is, we need to know it too."

He looked away for a few seconds. "What makes you think I have a clue about Beau Bradley's disappearance?"

"You walked away from us when we met the crew out in the roundhouse," Kathy said. "We realized something was off."

"Well, it wasn't me."

"What wasn't you?"

"I wasn't 'off,' and I had nothing to do with Beau Bradley's disappearance."

"Who said you did?" Kathy asked.

Jack glanced at her as if she were crazy. "You're here, aren't you?" He waved a hand in dismissal.

"How do you know something happened to him?" Heidi asked.

His face flushed with exasperation. "You're playing word games, Heidi—just like the old days. The guy disappeared. It has nothing to do with me."

"Then why did you say that?"

"Say what?"

Heidi was losing her patience. "That something happened."

Jack heaved a sigh. He reached over and pulled out a filtered menthol cigarette from the pack. He flicked his lighter on and lit up. "So, yes. There was . . . I saw . . . something weird." He stopped.

Suzanne's heart skipped a beat. "*Weird?* Like what? What did you see?"

He dragged on the cigarette, hard. His eyes whipped around the kitchen, as if searching for a way out.

He wants to say it, Suzanne figured, *but he can't spit it out.* Then . . .

"Blood."

Kathy gagged. Just the thought of the sticky stuff always made her sick to her stomach. *"Blood?"*

"Yup. Lots of it."

"Where?"

"Outside the back door of the roundhouse. It's just a normal, small door—same size as this one." He pointed to his apartment door. "A fire exit, not used a lot, but I snagged a key after I got there. I go out by myself on smoke breaks. There's a layer of sand on the ground there, butts right up to the building—we use sand in the railyard to sop up spilled oil, so we won't slip. It's all over the place. I spotted a big circle of discoloration at my feet—wine-colored, dark, still damp. Had no clue what it was until I stuck my hand in it."

"Blood?" Kathy asked again, feeling nauseous.

"Yup."

Heidi leaned closer to him, searching his face. "You're sure?"

"You bet I'm sure." He glanced at his right hand, making a face as he spread his fingers apart. "I had to wash the sticky stuff off. It was blood, all right."

Kathy's stomach flipped.

"How did you see in the dark?" Heidi asked.

"There's an outside security light above the back door."

"When did you find this?" Suzanne asked.

"Same day Beau disappeared," he replied. "Another welder called in sick, so they asked me to work overtime. That's not my thing, but I'm the backup guy. I'm usually outta there at three in the afternoon —that day I put in an extra six hours. Time and a half." He puffed on the cigarette and flicked ashes into the ashtray. "Some time after seven in the evening, I took a smoke break."

Heidi asked, "What did you think?"

"Think?" He looked at her and shrugged his shoulders. "Well— uh, I guess animal blood came to mind. We get bobcats, deer, skunks, you name it, wandering around Deception Gap. They even spotted a bear a few years ago. At first I thought maybe some animal had brought its prey there to eat." He paused for a few seconds. "But that made no sense. There's a ten-foot chain-link fence back of the roundhouse, and it's topped with rolls of razor wire. We keep lumber and other construction materials in the yard back there, and they fenced the area in to protect it from theft. I mean, it's darn near impossible to scale that fence—an animal would have to burrow under it, but that's a long shot . . ." He shook his head.

"So that's when you figured it was Beau's blood?" Suzanne asked.

"Heck no—never crossed my mind. At that stage I had no idea Beau had even disappeared."

"Until you figured it out," Kathy said. He blinked.

"When?" Suzanne asked.

Jack stared at her for a few seconds. "The next morning, I heard the scuttlebutt that Beau had vanished *after* he came to work. Now that's seriously weird. The blood popped right into my head. Then you showed up"—his eyes flicked over to Suzanne and Kathy. "When Ben said you were friends with Beau's mother, I couldn't help but notice Hank and Billy's reaction. I mean, those guys looked guilty as sin. That's when I got it."

"Got what?"

He blew a ring of smoke toward the low ceiling. "Somebody bumped Beau off."

"How do you know?"

"So much blood . . ."

Kathy caught her breath. "Who would do such a thing?"

Jack struggled a little to reply. "Well, that's a tough bunch of guys out there . . ."

Heidi blinked. "When you say, 'tough bunch of guys'. . . ?"

"No one messes with Hank and Billy."

"You figure they're responsible?"

He shrugged again. "Best guess I can come up with."

"C'mon, Jack," Heidi said. "Bumping him off? That's some serious stuff. What the heck could he have done to them?"

Jack glared at her. "Go ahead. You explain the blood."

Silence.

Kathy asked, "Why did you walk away from us in the roundhouse?"

"I figured Beau for dead," he replied, staring into his ashtray. "It tore me up inside. I liked the guy." He refused to make eye contact.

Suzanne changed tack. "Jack, we need a favor. Can we borrow your key to the back door of the roundhouse?"

The question startled him. "I dunno. Management wouldn't like it. They forgot all about my key. If anyone found out . . ."

It's not management he's worried about, Kathy realized. "We won't tell them."

"You can smoke anywhere," Suzanne urged, "and we'll get the key back to you—promise."

Jack exhaled sharply, reached into his jeans, pulled out a key chain, and twisted off a worn, corroded, silver-colored key. "Okay." He slid it across the kitchen table. His eyes locked onto Heidi as he covered the key with one hand. "It's our secret, right? I won't be reading about this in the newspaper?"

"Right," she replied. Then she winked at him and laughed. He grimaced. "Don't worry, Jack—I'll watch your back. In return, keep your wits about you. We need help figuring out the weirdness out there."

"Deal." He released the key, and Kathy scooped it up. "Just out of curiosity," she asked, "how many ways are there in and out of the roundhouse?"

"Just two," he replied. "The front doors and that fire exit at the back."

Suzanne had one last question too. "Jack, I need to ask you something."

"I'm already in deep water," he said with a deep sigh. "A little more can't hurt . . . I hope. What now?"

"Is there something illegal happening at Deception Gap?"

"You mean, other than murder?" he replied, with a touch of offhand humor that took the girls by surprise. "Nope. Nothing that I'm aware of."

A LATE-NIGHT CALL

S aturday night, after 11:00 p.m. All was quiet. The Jackson parents had retired shortly after ten.

Suzanne was right behind them. "I'm so bushed, I can't even see straight," she complained. "We've never had a day like this one. Night."

"Later," Tom replied, his eyes locked onto the TV. Whenever he needed to zone out, he flipped on his favorite old series, *The Twilight Zone*. This episode was about a guy who returns home to the town where he grew up, only to realize he has never been born. *Weird*. But good.

At 11:20 p.m., Tom's cell phone buzzed. *What the heck—who calls this late?* He glanced at the screen—Unknown Caller.

"Hello?"

"I'm looking for Tom Jackson," an older-sounding voice said.

Tom stood up, stammering, "Well—uh, yeah—this is Tom."

"Do you remember me, Fred Wilson?"

"Oh, sure, Fred, you bet I do. You work out at Deception Gap."

"Right. There's something gonna happen out here—tonight. And since you guys are watching this place for a reason, you need to check it out."

"When?"

"Now. Right now. And stay away from the employee parking lot —you don't want to bump into anyone. There's a left-hand turn onto a dirt road right before the lot. Take it, cut your headlights and follow the road to the end."

"Okay, we're on the way."

"When you park your car, you'll see the tower a couple hundred yards in front of you. I'll be watching for you. Don't come into the yard unless my flashlight clicks three times, got it? Three times."

"Got it."

"Okay. Good luck. Walk straight over to the tower and up the stairs. I'll be waiting for you." *Click.*

Ten minutes later, as they were hurrying down the highway with Tom at the wheel, Suzanne said, "When you woke me up, I thought I was dreaming. What about Kathy and Pete?"

"No time," Tom replied. "He wants us out there *now.*"

"But he didn't say why?"

"Nope. He said something's going on, he knows we're watching the place, and get out here."

"Now."

"Right now."

Suzanne sighed, watching the moonlit landscape whizz by until Tom turned onto the railyard's access road. "I told you he spotted me," she said. Then, "Do you realize how exhausted I'll be tomorrow? We never get any sleep. Why didn't he call Kathy and Pete?"

"Because I gave him my number, obviously. Think how much fun this is."

"Dream on."

Tom spotted the dirt road Fred had mentioned and hung a sharp left. He shut down his headlights as they bounced and bumped to a dead end, an eighth of a mile farther at most. He parked and cut the engine. "Okay, we're here. The tower lights are still on."

Suzanne glanced at her cell phone. It was 11:59 p.m. "Not for long."

The twins jumped out of the Chevy and stood in front of the car for a few seconds. The tower lights dimmed and Deception Gap's LEDs faded to minimal power all over the yard. A flashlight clicked on and off three times behind the tower's wraparound windows.

"There it is," Tom exclaimed. Excitement welled up inside him.

"And here we go," Suzanne said, leading the way. Running now on pure adrenaline, she had long forgotten about being tired.

It was a straight-line hike through the railyard to the control tower. They passed Mr. Z's offices and headed over to the tower's stairs. They climbed, as silently as possible, with a little apprehension. The tower door was wide open.

"Come on in," a quiet voice said from the darkness.

The twins' eyes adjusted within seconds. "Thanks for the invitation, Fred," Tom said. "You remember Suzanne?"

"Sure do," he said, shaking hands with the twins. His eyes ticked over to Suzanne. "We saw each other when you were on top of the eastern hill, didn't we?" He chuckled out loud.

"Yup, you busted me," she giggled.

"Well, that's when I figured out you were serious," he replied. "And I was glad to see it. This business with Beau really bothers me."

"Is that why you asked us out here?" Tom asked.

"In a way. I believe all of this is a big, ugly connecting circle. Come on over here." They stepped closer to the western windows as he pointed toward the cluster of four small, locked outbuildings that the mystery searchers had noticed during their first visit. "Guess who I spotted down there, just before I called you?"

Tom looked at him. "I—I haven't got a clue."

Suzanne shook her head.

"I'm not often looking in that direction," Fred explained. "No trains over here. And nobody working there—those little buildings have not been used in years. But I happened to glance over, surprised to spot Hank Rogers and Billy Booker sneaking around in the shadows."

"Which is . . . unusual?" Suzanne asked.

"Unusual?" Fred replied, his voice taut. "You bet your life it is. Their shift ended at three p.m. There's no reason for their presence anywhere in the yard, unless they're up to no good . . . and I'm certain they are."

"What makes you say that?" Suzanne asked.

"Well, there's no proof, that I admit," Fred replied. "But they must be skulking around out here, so long after the end of their shift, for a reason. Now here's the thing," he said, his voice dropping in an earnest, conspiratorial tone. "Those guys are up to something. Once before—a couple weeks back, one night when I stayed late to catch up on some paperwork—I passed them driving in on the access road after midnight on my way home. At the time, I figured they must have agreed to work some overtime. Never connected the dots . . . until Beau vanished. Somehow, his disappearance is connected to these two, I just feel it."

Fred had rushed his words out as if time were running out. "It's obvious to me they're waiting for my departure. I'll be out of here in a minute or two. That'll give *you* a chance to see what they're up to. After I leave, you glue yourselves to these windows. With the rail-yard's lights dimmed down, you'll have to keep your eyes peeled. It's pretty dark out there, I know, but your eyes adjust, believe me. You can use my binoculars too, right over there. I'm going to dim the lights in here all the way out"—he tapped a switch, plunging the deck into near total darkness—"so they can't see you if they happen to glance up here. You watch them—figure out what they're up to, what they're doing. Then"—he handed them a slip of paper—"call me. This is my cell number. Tonight. Any time. Tell me what's going on. Okay?"

The twins could hardly believe their own ears.

Suzanne replied, "We'll call you, Fred. For sure. You can count on us."

"Okay," he replied. He took a deep breath and shook hands with them both once more. "Good luck. I don't know how, but this might shed light on whatever happened to Beau. I feel so sorry for his mother. Good night." He turned and disappeared down the stairs.

Tom and Suzanne looked at one another in stunned silence.

"This is what Dad would call a break in the case," Tom breathed.

"You got that right."

Soon enough, they watched Fred Wilson's car exit the employee parking lot and travel west on the gravel road, heading toward the highway that would take him back to Prescott. No sooner had he disappeared when Suzanne spotted movement below. She grabbed Fred's binoculars for a closer look.

"Here they come, Tom. Fred was right. They're on a people mover." The mechanized two-person carrier headed toward the trains, two people in front. "And there's a good-size box on the back of it." She handed Tom the binoculars.

"Yup. Rogers and Booker, for sure. But I don't get it. Are they *shipping* a box? All this time we figured they were pirating stuff —*taking*, not sending."

"Stay tuned," his sister replied.

The men made their way to the first train and, turning left, traveled alongside it as they passed a dozen boxcars. The people mover stopped. Hank Rogers jumped out and walked over to the boxcar's sliding door.

"Look," Tom exclaimed. "I—I can't believe it! The guy's got a key: he's opened the door. Fred said no one had keys—until the end of the line."

Both men grabbed the box from the people mover and threw it up inside the boxcar. Then they jumped inside and yanked out another box. . . the same size. They carted the second box over to the people mover, setting it down—carefully —on the back. Then Rogers closed and locked the railcar's sliding door.

"It looks like they just *exchanged* identical boxes," Suzanne said excitedly. "What the heck . . ."

The people mover headed off toward the cluster of disused outbuildings, parking between two of them. Billy took off toward the employee parking lot as Hank Rogers opened the building's door and disappeared inside.

"Come on," Tom shouted. Let's see if we can get a better look at that box."

"Geez, Tom," Suzanne exclaimed, "those guys are dangerous. We'd better—"

Too late. Tom was already descending the stairs two at a time, with Suzanne trailing. They soon reached the row of outbuildings, tiptoeing silently. The people mover was sitting there in the shadows, right before their eyes. No sign of Hank Rogers. No Billy Booker either. But from somewhere, not far away, came the sound of muffled, hushed conversation.

"It's now or never," Suzanne hissed. She raced over to the vehicle and raised her cell phone, focusing on the box from close up. *Click.* A flash burst around them. *Oops.*

Footsteps.

"Hide!" Tom whispered. They disappeared into the darkness, crouching low against the wall of the next workshop.

Billy Booker had returned . . . and he wasn't alone.

"What was that?" a voice demanded. A familiar voice too. "Did you see a light flash?"

In the darkness, Suzanne squeezed her brother's arm. *"You know who that is, right?"* she whispered right in his ear.

"It can't be," Tom whispered back. *"It just can't be."*

"A light?" another voice replied. "Nope."

The sound of a slamming door jolted the Jackson's. Hank Rogers had returned. "Hey, Ben."

"Hey, yourself. Let's git, fast."

And then all three men slipped away into the night.

TOM AND SUZANNE WAITED A FEW MINUTES, HOLDING THEIR BREATH in the shadows, before daring to slip back to their car and jump into the front seat. Only then did Suzanne tap the Photos icon on her phone and open her most recent pic. She whistled out loud.

"What is it?" Tom asked. He still couldn't believe they had pulled it off.

"There're fancy graphics all over the box, a logo," Suzanne

replied. 'Simplicity Perfume, Singapore' . . . Just that, over and over again. . . *wait*. . . it also says '250 vials.'"

"Perfume!" Tom exclaimed. "What's the big deal about that. *Perfume?*"

"I've heard about that stuff, Tom," his sister replied. "Simplicity Perfume is the most expensive brand in the world today. All the high-end retailers sell it . . . for a thousand dollars an ounce. Or something just as ridiculous."

"Man, oh man! At that price, it'd better be out of this world."

"At that price, there could be a quarter million bucks' worth of product in that one box."

It was Tom's turn to whistle. "Pirates plunder."

"Including Ben Wright," Suzanne noted. And then, "Beau Bradley's blood is on Wright's hands, it appears, not to mention on the hands of his henchmen. These people must be responsible for the vanishing at Deception Gap."

She unrolled a little slip of paper and called Fred Wilson.

A DARK JOURNEY

Early on Sunday evening, Suzanne flipped a quarter into the air and let it plop onto the carpeted floor. "Heads!" she called out.

"Yahoo!" Pete shouted, giving his sister a high five. "We get the roundhouse, and you"—he pointed to the twins—"head to the top of the hill." He chortled, but Kathy didn't share his enthusiasm. Far from it.

"We'd better not get caught!" she snapped. "Those guys are dangerous."

"You worry too much."

"You don't worry enough."

Pete, still bummed out that he and Kathy had missed Saturday night's action, voiced his displeasure. "I still don't understand why you couldn't have at least texted," he groused, glancing over to the twins. "I mean, you figured out what the pirates were up to while we were fast asleep."

"And who's doing what, and to whom," Kathy added.

"Well, we don't have all the answers yet," Tom said. "Ben Wright's role is a riddle, that's for sure."

"Huh," Pete grunted.

"But we think they must be somehow swapping out the real stuff for counterfeit perfume," Suzanne said. "That would explain the switcheroo maneuver with the shipping boxes. But how do they sell the stolen perfume? What do they replace it with? And how come the retailers don't recognize the difference?"

Pete's grumbling tapered off after a challenge from Suzanne.

"Remember Beau?" she said. "We need to find the guy—or what's left of him. That's more important than anything else."

"What did Detective Ryan say after you told him?" Kathy asked.

Suzanne giggled. "He said, 'Perfume? You gotta be kidding me.'"

Tom cracked up. "He got it after we told him the stuff's worth a thousand bucks an ounce."

Suzanne said, "So did Dad."

After comparing notes, the foursome decided to split into two teams. The Brunellis would attack the roundhouse at midnight—in mere hours—sneaking through its interior to the tiny back door, the one revealed by Jack. It was, they realized, the only feasible way to secure their objective: to retrieve a sample of the dried blood he said they would find there.

"Wear a glove so you don't contaminate the stuff, and slip it into this evidence bag," Tom instructed his friends. He produced a small, see-through plastic bag. It was truly convenient that the twins' father was the chief of police.

Suzanne said, "We only need a tiny amount. Prescott City Police can run a DNA test on it and compare the blood sample against Beau's mom's. If there's a match . . ." She didn't finish. She didn't have to. It was an awful thing to contemplate.

Meanwhile, the twins would trek to the eastern hilltop over-looking Deception Gap and dispatch the drone into the night sky. Just in case the pirates returned to swap out some more pricey merchandise.

"At the same time, we'll watch your back," Tom said, glancing over at his best friends. A full moon would ensure plenty of visibility despite the railyard's dimmed exterior lighting.

In the twins' world, their assignment was a win-win. Piloting the drone was always a blast. And flying at night? *Cool.*

TOM AND SUZANNE DROPPED THE BRUNELLI'S AT THE SIDE OF THE access road to Deception Gap, a couple hundred yards away from the parking lot. They chorused a hushed "Bye!" and wished them luck before Tom pulled a tight U-turn and the Chevy disappeared.

Silence descended over the lonely landscape. The ever-present cicadas chirped in the night. The air smelled cool and clean. In the distance, the railyard's intermittent hammering drummed on.

The Brunellis had arrived half an hour early; the plan was for the two teams to launch simultaneously. While they waited, Pete and Kathy huddled in tall roadside grass.

"Are we sure about this?" Kathy asked.

"We're never sure of anything."

"Very helpful, thank you."

Time dragged until Pete glanced at his cell phone for the umpteenth time: 11:55. "Let's go." No way could he conceal his excitement.

The siblings avoided the road itself and hustled along in the ditch. Not that they'd run into anyone else in the middle of the night. *But hey, you never know,* Kathy thought. Headlights presented a genuine threat, coming or going.

At midnight—their planned arrival time—the yard's artificial daylight began its nightly sixty-second fade to its minimal setting.

"Wilson's on his way," Pete warned. "Get ready to hit the dirt."

Soon enough, a four-door sedan came rattling along the gravel road, its headlights bouncing into the night. They buried themselves in knee-high grass until the vehicle had passed.

"We're up, Kathy," Pete urged.

At the entry to the parking lot, they circled around behind the all-seeing security camera, trekking off into high country before slipping onto the premises. Next, they passed the stationmaster's darkened offices and, ducking low—*Just in case*—they glided over the gloomy, silent railyard. The workshops served as cover as they slipped from one to another, guarding against any sign of danger in their quest for . . .

Blood! A shiver ran down Kathy's spine as she pictured the icky red stuff sinking into pale sand. A sick feeling flooded the pit of her stomach. Was it the blood, or the danger of the unknown? She wasn't sure which, but it was far too late to turn back now anyway. They trekked onward, Pete in the lead. *It's like he's on a picnic,* Kathy thought.

The roundhouse loomed dead ahead. They jogged over and slipped through its giant front doors, stepping into the cavernous interior. Deep inside, near the center of the vast space, a few bright work lights were focused downward from high overhead, leaving most of the surrounding interior in shadow. A radio played raucous rock music that echoed, revealing the workers' location: almost straight ahead, a bit to the right, hidden from sight by the locomotives they were working on.

"Same as last time," Kathy hissed. "We go left, Pete."

They pivoted noiselessly and headed into the shadows, Kathy in front, hugging the inside of the roundhouse's curving wall, feeling their way forward. It was slow going.

Kathy turned when she heard Pete fall behind her. He landed almost silently, both hands extended in front of him. He must have tripped over something.

"You okay?" Kathy whispered.

"Yeah, but this isn't working—there's nothing but ink in front of us. I think we should light it up a bit."

"You sure?"

Pete smothered the back of his cell phone with one hand, then fired up its flashlight. He parted two fingers, allowing a tiny sliver of light to escape.

The duo picked up speed, still hugging the building's interior wall, arcing their way silently toward the rear of the roundhouse around heaps of equipment on the floor. At one stage they passed a ghostly locomotive—like a giant beast deserted on the outbound tracks—before slipping under the huge legs of an overhead crane.

Even with a flashlight lighting the way, hazards were plentiful. It was Kathy's turn to trip next, and she hit the concrete floor hard, with a muffled thud. *That hurt!*

Pete reached down with an outstretched arm, helping her to her feet. Neither one uttered a sound.

This is what happens when you lose a coin toss, Kathy ruminated.

The familiar hammering started up—so much louder in the enclosed space—but quickly faded. The siblings heard men talking and shouting; there was a smattering of bad language and laughter too. Once, the sound of purposeful footsteps drew alarmingly close, followed by the scraping noise of some heavy piece of equipment being dragged across the concrete floor. The Brunellis stopped in their tracks, holding their breath, and slid closer to the floor. A minute passed. Then more hammering, starting and stopping. More laughter.

They continued, slow and steady. At last a doorframe materialized, just a few feet in front of them.

"There it is!" Kathy whispered: a windowless, metal-clad door with a push bar. They paused, scanning for threats, before she eased the key that Jack had loaned them into the lock. She turned the key, left . . . then right. *"It doesn't work!"* she hissed.

Pete tried with the same result. "Oh, man," he muttered. He stopped and looked to his sister. "What now?"

"Try pulling or pushing the door a little, then turning the key," Kathy suggested.

Pete pulled the door toward him; it gave maybe a quarter inch. He turned the key to the left. *Success!* He wanted to cheer. "How did you know?"

"I didn't. The school's after-hours locker room door does that too."

Pete pressed the door's push bar slowly, easing the door open with one hip. It squealed softly, but to the Brunellis, the sound was like a salvo of artillery fire. They slipped through, then Kathy pushed the door behind them, leaving it slightly ajar—just in case. The resulting muted squeal caused them to freeze a few seconds, waiting and watchful.

Lord, Kathy thought, *I hope no one heard that.*

They found themselves under the glare of a weak outside security light, slanting toward them from high up the wall. Just a few yards away was the chain-link fence mentioned by Jack, topped with razor wire, enclosing racks of lumber pyramiding six-feet high. Pete fell to his knees and unleashed his phone's flashlight to its full beam. Even out in the open air, released from the threat of discovery inside the roundhouse, he spoke in a hushed tone. "See anything?"

He swept the light from the door outward in widening arcs, creating myriad pockets of shadow in the uneven sand-strewn ground.

"That won't work," Kathy said, giggling. She turned on her cell phone flashlight and illuminated the ground straight down at her feet. "See? No shadows."

Pete stood up and tried it. "You're right. I'll go left, you go right."

Seconds later, Kathy called out, "Bingo!"

Pete rushed over to find his sister gently brushing and blowing a thin top layer of clean sand away to uncover a jaggedly outlined, roundish patch of sand. Stained a rusty brown, almost a foot in diameter, it glared up at them in the blaze of their phone flashlights. She was trying hard not to disturb the stain itself—to not even touch it. "I saw a bit of red, she said. Someone obviously tried to cover this up—"

"But not well enough to hide if from us," Pete said.

"Well, from *me*," Kathy said.

"That's gotta be it," Pete murmured, too moved by the site of human blood to take the bait, for once.

"*E-e-ew.*" Kathy pulled the evidence bag from her jeans pocket and handed it to her brother. "You do it. I'm can't stand to touch that stuff."

"It's old, all dried up."

"So what! It's still blood." Tiny prickles traveled up Kathy's arms.

Pete fell to one knee, lay the evidence bag flat on top of the sand, and pressed a finger gently into the center of the discoloration. Through the plastic, the sand felt cold, gritty, and a little damp—which meant nothing; at night, he realized, all the sand would be damp and clammy. He used the bag to scoop up an ounce or so, making sure none of it touched his fingers.

At that moment, a voice rang out from the far side of the fence. "Hey! What's going on there? *HEY!*"

PIRATE ACTION

A fter dropping off the Brunellis, the twins circled around to the far side of the eastern hill. Tom parked at the base of a familiar dirt road that dead-ended at the trailhead.

"Perfect flying weather," Suzanne said. A gentle breeze passed over them. They pulled out two cases from the Chevy's trunk, both marked FRAGILE—HANDLE WITH CARE, setting them down beside the car. Then they unpacked a handheld controller, extra battery, and the drone itself.

"It always amazes me how light this thing is," said Tom. He tossed the empty cases back into the trunk. "You ready, Suzie?"

"Uh-huh. Let's do it."

Fifteen minutes later, the twins reached the hill's summit, just in time to watch the railyard fade to its dim, 10-percent lighting. Tom positioned the bird on a large, flat area while Suzanne fired up the controller. They watched as Fred Wilson's vehicle—headlights blazing in the night—pulled away from the parking lot and headed toward Prescott.

The plan was to wait until twelve-thirty, hoping that thirty minutes would be enough time for Pete and Kathy to reach their objective . . . *and* safely exit the roundhouse.

The twins rested on the brow of the hill, dangling their feet over the side. In the distance, light emerged from the roundhouse doors and seeped through the grimy windows, while near darkness shrouded the rest of the railyard. The familiar hammering started up more than once, but soon faded away.

The waxing moon danced through a layer of dense clouds, silvering the landscape for short bursts, then disappearing again behind veils of gloom. The twins could see no activity anywhere.

They chatted. "Our biggest problem is time," Suzanne said.

Airtime was thirty minutes—"Way too short" they agreed—after which the drone required a battery change. *That* was problematic. "Puts us out of business for a few minutes," Tom complained.

"No kidding," Suzanne said. "We could easily miss something." There was little choice; all they could do was keep a sharp eye on the controller's power indicator and bring the bird home before its juice ran too low.

Suzanne pulled out her cell phone and texted Kathy: *What's up?* No answer.

Tom, the club's team leader, had learned to fly the aircraft to record school events. The sensitive on-board camera streamed live HD video footage to the controller and any connected smart wireless devices. In the space of two years, he had become the technology team's most experienced remote pilot. He often worked with his sister at school; tonight, it was her turn to pilot.

He glanced at his cell phone. "*Showtime.*"

Suzanne grabbed the controller, and the twins jumped to their feet. To be safe, she touched the lighting control panel, shutting down the bird's piercing headlights. No sense alerting unwanted eyes. With a whirring sound like an angry beehive, the aircraft lifted and soared away, rapidly climbing to three hundred feet, a recommended altitude that placed the drone well above power lines, trees, buildings, and other potential obstacles.

The moon emerged from behind the cloud cover. On their screens the twins enjoyed a scenic nighttime view of the railyard— and at three hundred feet, the acreage rolled out before them. There were three lines of boxcars, stationary on the snake-like tracks, each line headed by a locomotive. The train closest to the roundhouse had two of the iron beasts harnessed together.

Suzanne piloted the aircraft to offer an eastward view of the yard. There wasn't a soul in sight, zero activity.

Glued to the live stream on his cell phone app, Tom suggested circling the entire railyard to include a view from the west. "The image is clean as anything. Good visibility, and you're getting super video."

"There's nothing out here," Suzanne replied, "and we're burning up the juice." She glanced at her power gauge. Sixteen minutes had ticked away. "Let's get closer and circle the roundhouse. Kathy and Tom should be on their way out by now."

"Do it."

Suzanne piloted the drone across the yard, from east to west, and dropped a hundred feet for a better view of the roundhouse's entrance. *Nothing.* "I'll start the circle now." She sent the unit right and began a circle, slow and steady, all the way back to the starting point.

"Hey, check out that chain-link fence," she said.

"It's a tall one," Tom said. "Must be ten feet high." Just a guess, he knew—judging distance and height on the video feed was difficult, more so at night. "That razor wire looks dangerous."

"Ten feet is right—that's what Jack told us," Suzanne said. "Wait a sec— *Look!*" A dim outdoor security light revealed an open door.

Tom searched his screen. "So they made it there, out that rear exit, and now they're on the way back."

"Well, yeah, but—they didn't close the door? That's not right."

"Maybe it was open when they reached it."

"That's not what Jack told us to expect."

The twins glanced at each other, baffled. Suzanne pushed the bird closer to the fenced-in area, dropping another fifty feet, to one hundred and fifty feet above the ground. Nothing but piles of lumber and an open back door that stood out like a flashing red light.

"Not good," Suzanne said. "I'll keep going." She glanced at the drone's power gauge: twenty-two minutes of juice had evaporated. It felt like less time had passed. "Eight minutes left."

As Suzanne piloted the drone along the western side of the roundhouse, alarm bells began ringing in her head. Two flashlight beams had emerged from somewhere up front, bobbing up and down, arcing along close to the structure's exterior wall.

"Flashlights!"

"Yeah, got it," Tom said. "They're looking for Pete and—"

Just at that moment, outlined by the silvery moonlight, Tom saw the unmistakable silhouettes of first Kathy, then Pete wriggle out through a low window and drop to the ground about halfway between the building's front and rear doors. They raced away from the building.

Tom shouted, "Look, it's them!"

"Yes!" Suzanne cried out. "And those two guys are after them."

"They're heading for open country," Tom said, his voice strained. "Good for them. Flip the headlights on."

Suzanne touched the lighting panel on the controller, turning on the drone's piercing headlights. "I can move closer, light the way for Pete and Kathy. There're no obstacles out there."

"No! Drop the bird down and freak them out!"

"Freak them out?"

"Heck, yeah, the pursuers! We've got to save the Brunellis!"

MINUTES EARLIER, PETE HAD YANKED THE HEAVY FIRE EXIT DOOR open wider and torn into the darkness of the roundhouse, Kathy hard on his heels, neither one muting their flashlights now. They ran as fast as they could, flashlight beams arcing wildly back and forth as they skirted around the same equipment they had avoided only minutes earlier.

Remember what happened to Beau Bradley, Kathy thought. *Wait— don't think. Run!*

85

She tripped, catching herself as Pete reached back to break her fall, grabbing her by a shoulder. "You okay?" His voice was raspy.

"Define okay."

"Keep going."

They started off again, Kathy now taking the lead. From somewhere ahead came voices—loud, insistent, shouting. *Uh-oh. Trouble.* The guy who had yelled at them must have ratted them out, phoned or texted his accomplices—maybe the gang even had two-way radios. Still, the voices weren't close—yet. No imminent threat—but for how long?

Something dawned on Pete. He began slowing down. *Of course!* The pirates wouldn't have to chase intruders. This was *their* territory. They knew it well. There were only two ways in or out: the narrow back door, *with nowhere to go*, or the vast front doors. The pirates simply had to wait for them there—Pete stopped, bending over to catch his breath.

Kathy turned to her brother in alarm. "What are you doing?" she hissed. *"What's wrong?"*

15

A NARROW ESCAPE

Pete straightened up and moved closer to his sister. "If we keep going," he wheezed, "they'll get us for sure . . . trap us when we try to rush through the front doors. We'd better turn back and take our chances. Let's try scaling that fence."

Kathy felt almost ready to slug him. "You can't be seri—"

At that moment, a strange, disembodied voice—subdued and insistent at the same time—whispered from the darkness: "The windows—you just passed them. Go back to the windows. *It's your only chance.*"

"Who the heck is that?" Kathy said. "And where . . .?"

Doesn't matter. In a heartbeat—*Not a second to waste!*—the siblings spun around and tore back, fifty yards at most. A vast expanse of grimy panes of glass materialized, each only about two feet square, embedded in the roundhouse's curved wall and all but invisible. The two played the beams of their flashlights desperately across the soiled surface—so filthy, the windows were virtually nonreflective.

"Check it out!" Pete exclaimed. The center bottom pane of glass, right about at waist level, sported a side-crank handle. The window looked as though it would offer a gap large enough to squeeze through if—*if*—it would open. Pete grabbed the handle and tried cranking it. "Oh, man. This thing hasn't moved in years."

He arced his flashlight around the floor, executing a complete circle, looking for any—*There!* A short metal rod. "We've got one shot at this, Kathy. If it doesn't work, we'll smash the glass." He whacked the handle, hard.

The bang reverberated, echoing through the cavernous space. *"You'll wake the dead,"* Kathy hissed in protest.

But the crank had moved. Pete grabbed it and yanked hard. It turned, ever so slightly, tilting the pane a few degrees outward. He hauled on the handle a second time, cranking it open a bit more. It took almost an entire agonizing minute—an eternity—for the window to open as wide as it could, to about forty-five degrees. All the while, Kathy guarded her brother's back, her flashlight off, wary and watching.

"Go, Kathy, *go!*"

She slipped through the opening and dropped to the ground, breathing hard again as she tore away from the structure.

Pete was right behind her. "Move it! They'll be after us for sure."

"More joy—*flashlights,*" Kathy blurted, trying her best not to sound panicked. "And they're coming our way." *Two flashlights, two men?*

"Our only hope is the open country, let's bug outa here!" Pete said. They pivoted to the right.

Their pursuers had closed to maybe fifty yards, their heavy boots hammering the hard earth.

A voice shouted, "Hey, hold up there! We just want to talk to you."

Sure, Kathy's mind raged. *Like you wanted to "talk" to Beau Bradley!*

"Faster," Pete breathed.

All at once, the pounding footsteps behind the Brunellis halted.

"What the—?" a man's voice said.

The siblings slowed to a stop and turned around.

Another voice shouted, "A drone!"

More words, jumbled, unintelligible. And then, just like that, it was over. Their pursuers had melted into the night.

Pete and Kathy looked at each other and burst out laughing.

"Look!" Pete shouted. Kathy followed his gaze. The bird tilted toward them, pointing downward at a crazy angle. They leapt up and down, waving at the camera. Pete gestured in the direction of the gravel access road that led out of Deception Gap. The drone rocked its nose up and down, nodding: *Message received.* Then it shot skyward and disappeared.

"WAS THAT GREAT, OR WHAT!" TOM EXCLAIMED.

"Whoo-hoo!" his sister shouted. Glancing down at the controller, her tone became instantly graver. "We've got less than four minutes left."

Tom asked, "Where did the pirates go?"

Suzanne piloted the bird back along the exterior wall of the roundhouse and rotated it so that the camera had a view of the front of the structure. Nothing. She turned the drone to scan up along the row of darkened outbuildings. "We lost them."

"We sure did," Tom said. "Wouldn't you wonder where the heck...?"

Suzanne touched a shortcut command on the controller: Home. "Let's go find Kathy and Pete. We're done."

"We're done, all right," Tom replied grimly. "In fact, we're busted. Now they know we're on to them."

MEANWHILE, THE BRUNELLIS TREKKED OUT FROM THE RAILYARD, circling behind and well clear of the security camera and retracing their steps along the ditch at the side of the access road. They knew it would take time for the twins to pack up, hike back down the hill, and drive to the access road. Still, they hustled, trying to put distance between themselves and the pirates.

At one stage, Pete stopped and locked eyes with his sister. "Who warned us? Who told us to head for the windows?"

"You don't know?"

He bristled. "You do?"

"Well, think about it. Who gave us a key to the back door?"

"Oh, yeah. Got it. Of course. Could only be him. But where did his voice come from?"

"No clue," Kathy said. "But that was Jack Riley. We owe that guy, big-time."

16

PROOF POSITIVE

F our tired but excited mystery searchers hustled into Detective Ryan's office early on Monday morning and handed him a ziplocked plastic bag.

"What is it?" he asked.

"Blood!" Pete replied, as if he had just scored a touchdown.

"Beau's blood," Kathy added. "Right where Jack said it would be."

"No kidding," the investigator said, eyebrows raised. He held the bag up to the ceiling lights. "I'll send it to the lab. And I'll ask Beau's mom to come in for a DNA swab." He glanced over at them. "Have any trouble getting it?"

All four heads shook back and forth.

"Nothing we couldn't handle," Suzanne replied. The foursome had agreed not to reveal too many details.

"Another late night?"

"You bet," Pete replied.

The detective's eyes searched their faces. "And?"

Kathy hesitated before picking up the story. "Well . . . after we exited the roundhouse, two guys gave chase."

"Like, *right* after us," Pete said. "But Tom and Suzanne had the drone above us, watching our backs."

"Thank goodness," Kathy said. "It made all the difference."

"The bird freaked them out," Tom confirmed. "They took off, and we never saw them again."

"Rogers and Booker?" Detective Ryan asked.

"Nope," Pete answered. "First time we ever saw these guys."

Ryan twisted in his chair toward the twins. "Does the Chief know about Simplicity Perfume?"

"Yes, sir, we told him this morning."

The detective glanced at his watch. "After I received your text, I contacted Simplicity Perfume's offices in Singapore. Fortunately for me, they speak perfect English. They're having one of their U.S. representatives meet the train in Denver—about right now, in fact. I asked them to examine the shipment and test the perfume for authenticity."

"Perfect," Suzanne declared.

"Exactly what we wanted," Tom said. "Can they get into the boxcar?"

"I imagine they'll cut the lock if they have to," Detective Ryan replied. "What about the chase last night? Did you fill in the Chief?"

"Uh-huh," Suzanne answered. She didn't elaborate, and Tom added not a word.

The detective nodded. "Okay . . . all right." Even though it obviously wasn't. "So it appears that two of our primary suspects have helpers."

"Fellow plundering pirates," Pete said, grinning.

"I'll pass that info to the officer on the ground," the detective muttered, almost to himself. He rested his chin in both hands, blinking like crazy, and disappeared into his thoughts for a few seconds. "By now, they've figured out someone's on to them, obviously. I think it's time we shut this operation down."

"We were hoping for one more run out there," Tom said earnestly.

"When?"

"Tonight."

"*Tonight?* I dunno. After your experience last night—*whatever that was* . . . they'll be on guard."

"Yes, sir. But this could be our last chance."

Suzanne weighed in. "Here's the thing: we have some idea what the pirates are doing out there . . . but we have *no idea* what happened to Beau. If you round them up now, we might never find Beau's body. What if they don't crack when you question them? That would be a terrible blow to his mother."

Kathy added, "She might never discover the fate of her son."

"Or his body," Pete said.

The detective drummed his fingers on the desk.

"It's worth a try, sir," Tom prompted.

Seconds ticked by in slow motion. "Okay. One more shot, and that's it. I'll alert the undercover officer—you'll have another watcher out there. But *be careful.* These guys are dangerous."

"We will," Pete said, his spirits soaring. *Boy, is this fun or what?*

An hour later, Mrs. Bradley walked into the police station to give a DNA sample—a simple cheek swab. It would take a few hours to confirm a match, if indeed there was one. The mystery searchers detailed the previous night's adventures for Beau's mother as tactfully as they could.

The idea that Beau's blood might have appeared in the sand brought tears to the woman's face. "Such a good boy, what a terrible thing."

"It's not for certain," Kathy said.

"Maybe not, but it sure doesn't look good, does it?" She wiped the tears from her eyes and blew her nose. "And all of that just for perfume?"

Minutes later, the Chief came out of a meeting to receive his update from the young detectives. He wasn't too enthusiastic about the prospect of another midnight excursion either. "This is getting dangerous."

"Our undercover officer will be on site," Detective Ryan assured his boss. "And I'll stay close for backup too."

Heidi Hoover called—nothing could keep her away from a breaking story. Kathy put her on speaker. "Wow, perfume! Who would have ever imagined? Are they swapping it out, or what?"

"That we don't know . . . yet," Suzanne replied.

When they got to the blood part, Heidi went ballistic. "Beau's blood? You found a sample? *All right.* Zimmerman's heading for the slammer." And when she discovered they were heading back to the railyard that same night, she was beside herself. "Can I come?"

"No!" Detective Ryan replied curtly from across his desk. "There are already too many cooks in the kitchen."

Late in the day, the lab texted results of the DNA test. A match. Mrs. Bradley had only one child. The blood had to be Beau's.

TRAPPED

T hat night, just after midnight, everything worked fine—until it didn't.

The idea, Tom said, was "to go to ground"—literally. No more drones or spying from a distance. No bugs, cameras, or any other electronic surveillance, either. Sure, they had all been effective in previous adventures. But here . . . no.

"It's our last chance," he argued. "We need to get close enough to *listen* to them, try to get a lead on Beau's body. Because if we fail . . ."

"We're toast," Suzanne said.

"We'd better not get caught," Kathy grumbled. She didn't like the idea. Toast or no toast.

"We'll be fine," Suzanne said. "There's safety in numbers."

Pete was all in. "We'll use the boxcars for cover. Those things are enormous."

"If there's no action by the trains—and there probably *won't* be— we'll sneak into the roundhouse," Tom advised. "We'll spread out inside and surveil the crew, watching and listening. We need to come up with *something.*"

And it worked, at first. After entering the railyard, the mystery searchers scurried from one shadowy hiding place to another, crouching low to cross the tracks, keeping a low profile. And silent. *So silent.* It seemed like forever, but they soon reached the first train, arriving toward its front. They circled a pair of locomotives, harnessed together, ready to lead. Behind the two iron beasts sat dozens of boxcars, waiting for the morning run, stretching out along a straight line in the moonlight.

No movement—not another soul anywhere.

Tom whispered, "Suzanne and I will head down this side of the train. You guys take the other side."

"No way," Suzanne hissed. "Kathy and I go together."

"That's not safe," Tom argued.

"Listen, hotshot," his sister retorted. "We're capable of looking after ourselves. Right, Kathy?"

"Right. We go together."

"Super," Pete said, thumbs up. Either way was fine with him. *"Let's go."*

The girls slipped between two boxcars around to the west side of the train and headed out. Tom grumbled to himself but led the way along the east side. Wary and cautious, the boys kept track of their sisters by glancing under the boxcars and listening for the sound of footsteps. The two pairs kept even with each other, slipping past the boxcars in unison. Pete counted to himself: *Twenty-two . . . twenty-three . . . twenty-four—*

From nowhere, masked men jumped from the top of the boxcars, swinging chains, screaming and cursing.

"Duck!" Tom shouted. Too late. Pete took a chain on the arm, a crushing blow that sent him reeling. Tom caught sight of the girls between two boxcars, racing away.

"Move it!" Pete screamed in pain. The boys bolted in the opposite direction, back to where they had come from, sliding under one boxcar and hurtling past another, faster and faster, until they outran the pursuers . . . then up, up into the front locomotive's cabin to catch their breath.

Pete's arm ached, big-time. He touched it gingerly. *Ouch.*

That was when Tom phoned Suzanne, three worrisome times,

until she finally answered. Soon, the boys hit the ground once more, working their way toward her, despite whatever danger might lurk in wait for them, counting the boxcars again as they passed.

A woman screamed, a shattering wail that penetrated the night before cutting off.

"What the heck?" Pete blurted as they ground to a standstill. *"Was that—?"*

The boys broke into a run, hoping against hope that Suzanne was only seconds away.

The boxcars whipped by faster. No Suzanne. Still, they silently counted: *Twenty-one . . . twenty-two . . . twenty-three—*

"See that?" Pete whispered. A heavy, two-foot length of chain lay beside one boxcar, dropped in a weirdly tidy circle. "I bet anything that's the one that got me." He touched his arm for the umpteenth time. No sign of the pirates. And still no Suzanne. "What now?"

"Keep going," Tom said. "We're almost—"

A huge, hairy arm imprisoned Tom from behind, wrapping around him like an octopus tentacle. Another hand covered his mouth. He couldn't move a muscle, nor make a sound. Pete suffered a similar fate: one arm locked his elbows tight against his torso, a hand clamped his mouth shut.

The one who had grabbed Pete whispered, *"Be quiet. We're on your side."* A woman's voice! She slowly released Pete's mouth.

"What the—!" he started. Her hand muzzled him again.

"Shut up," she hissed.

Pete twisted around in her grip to look at her. *"Olivia?"*

"Uh-huh," she replied with a smile. "That's *Officer Brady* to you, young man."

Tom's captor released him from his steely grip and dropped his hand away from Tom's face. Even in the darkness, Tom could make out the man's face. "Boss Zimmerman?"

"Who'd you expect, Santa Claus?" the big man growled.

Tom was speechless, but Pete was never at a loss for words. "They captured Kathy, but we were looking for Suzanne."

"Uh-oh," Officer Brady exclaimed. She looked toward Boss

Zimmerman. "That's not good. So the scream we heard must've come from Suzanne. They got her."

Tom said, "I think it's time we called for reinforcements."

"Detective Ryan is just minutes away," the officer said. She pulled a two-way radio from her back pocket and hit the talk button. "We've got problems, sir. I think it's time to move in. They've captured the two girls."

There was a slight buzzing sound before the investigator's voice replied. "Okay, I'll set it up . . . Ten minutes, and we'll lock everything down."

Boss Zimmerman didn't talk—he growled. "What are you doing out here, anyway?"

Pete replied. "We're looking for information on where the pirates buried Beau Bradley."

"Buried him? If that's true, you're playing a dangerous game."

"We're moving this case forward," Tom said firmly. "We found Beau's blood behind the roundhouse."

"His *blood?*" Zimmerman's exclaimed. "How do you—" He stopped. In the distance, they heard a car door slam—four doors, in fact. A vehicle's ignition fired up. "Someone's pulling out of the parking lot."

Pete grinned in the dark. "Pirates abandoning the sinking ship."

Tom pulled his cell phone from his back jeans pocket. He clicked on the GPS app. "We might get lucky." And, a few seconds later, he confirmed it. "Hank Rogers—it's his SUV."

"How do you know?" Officer Brady asked.

"We attached a GPS tracker to it," Pete replied. "It allows us to follow him anywhere. Look."

Tom held the screen up. It displayed a local map with the blinking icon of a car traveling away from Deception Gap along the access road.

Zimmerman's voice softened. "Well, I'll be darned."

"It was Pete's idea," Tom said, giving his buddy credit. "Officer Brady, can I borrow your two-way for a sec?" Tom radioed Detective Ryan. "Four pirates are heading your way. We think they're fleeing—the game is up and they know it."

"I'll have a welcoming committee waiting for them," the detective replied curtly.

Pete's impatience mounted. "What about the girls?"

18

THE HUNT

"Beau's blood . . ." Zimmerman repeated. He seemed fixated on the words. "Are these rogue men responsible for his demise?"

"We think so, sir," Pete replied.

"Oh, Lord, was I ever wrong about that fine young man. What now?"

"The girls," Tom urged again. "We need to find them."

"Let's head to the roundhouse," Mr. Z said. "We'll turn this place upside down."

Sirens wailed in the distance.

Soon, under Mr. Z's direction, a posse of ten railyard workers was turning the gigantic structure inside out, with Tom and Pete helping every step of the way. They turned all the work lights up high to explore four locomotives and the vast floor beneath and all around them. Half a dozen police officers soon joined in the hunt. The shift foreman pulled out a key for the back door. Nothing out there. No clues. And no sign of the girls.

Zimmerman shouted, "Let's move out to the yard!"

Officer Brady caught up with the boys. "You don't have a 'Find My Friends' app on either of your phones?"

"Sure do," Tom replied. "Both of us. But the girls' cell phones must be turned off. We already tried."

"Too bad they weren't carrying one of your GPS trackers," she said, winning a smile from Pete.

"No kidding," Tom replied. "That would be a—" He stopped.

"What?" Pete asked.

"Is it possible?" Tom pulled out his cell phone and tapped on the icon for a fitness app. When it had opened, he keyed in an alphanumeric code. *Easy.* No matter how many times he warned her not to, his sister always used the same password. "Look at that," he exclaimed, holding up his phone.

Pete, Officer Brady, and Mr. Z clustered around. Tom's phone showed a stylized map of the railyard, with a dotted path of footsteps stitched across it.

Zimmerman stared over Tom's shoulder. "What are we looking at?"

"Suzie runs a fitness app on her phone," Tom explained. "She says it helps her stay in shape. I logged in as her just now. So it's like we're looking at *her* phone. That's her trail, tonight, in the Cloud."

"There's a break in her path there, opposite that workshop—at the last boxcar in the train," Pete said, his voice rising with excitement. "I bet she hid up there for a bit. Then, look, she walks alongside the train again, stops twice: *danger!* And then, *here*"—he jabbed the screen with an index finger—"you can see her steps churning around in place—"

"That must be where they grabbed her!" Tom said.

At the bottom of the image there flashed: *Total: 389 steps, 0.47 miles.*

Tom held the screen up. "What is that, sir? That building—where her path ends. What is it?"

Mr. Z eyeballed the image, trying to make sense of the tiny map. Seconds ticked by before he muttered, almost to himself, "They locked her up."

"I—I don't understand," Tom said, trying to read his face.

"That building hasn't been in use for the better part of a century,"

Mr. Z explained. "It's a railroad jail, built in the early nineteen-hundreds."

"*A jail?*" the boys chorused.

"Correct. The jail cell is still there, upstairs, on the second level, all bricked up. No windows. It's the perfect place to hide someone." Zimmerman lurched away, shouting, "This way, men!"

Soon, the entire posse had surrounded a squat, two-story building. A thick chain secured the front door handle, held in place by a padlock. Pete grabbed the lock and shook it—hard. "No way!" he called out.

Tom glanced at Boss Zimmerman. "Do you have a key?"

He ignored the question. "Leonard," he shouted to a foreman. "We need bolt cutters."

The boys circled the building, searching for another way in. But heavy boards, secured by thick screws, barricaded the ground-floor windows. The exterior second floor was nothing but brick.

Leonard soon returned with the biggest bolt cutters Tom had ever seen. "This will make quick work of the chain," he said. The man's strength was enormous. There was a loud *snap!*—and the chain fell to the ground.

Pete yanked the heavy door open. The boys, Officer Brady, and Boss Zimmerman rushed in, followed by a throng of police officers and railyard workers. Cell phone flashlights blazed, arcing through empty space, displaying nothing but a stairway leading to a second story.

"Anybody here?" Pete yelled.

"Upstairs!" someone screamed back.

Kathy.

"We're here!" Suzanne shouted.

The boys took the old wooden stairs two at a time. Pete glanced back once, shocked to see a gun in Officer Brady's hand. Boss Zimmerman trailed, glowering.

Upstairs, the band of rescuers came face to face with the two girls, their hands wrapped around the wrong side of the steel bars of the jail's cell, their faces shining with excitement.

Tom walked right up to his sister and admonished her. "Next time, you'd better listen to me!" He gave her a high five through the bars anyway.

"Shut up," she replied. "Get us out of here. And hand us our cell phones. The pirates threw them in the corner behind you."

"Okay, got it. That explains why your fitness app trail ends here," Tom said.

"Wait a sec," Pete said. He pointed his flashlight into the far corner of the cell. Something had moved in the dark. "Who's that?"

"That?" his sister teased. She giggled. "Oh, you mean *him*. Say hello to our newest friend, Mr. Beauford Bradley."

19

GAME CHANGERS

"You gotta be kidding!" Pete exclaimed. "Beau's alive? *That's him?* I mean, you're him, it's you, sir—you're Beau?"

Tom stepped closer and peered between the bars. "Great to meet you, Beau. I'm Tom, Suzie's brother. Your mother will be awfully glad to see you."

"Yes . . . Kathy told me," Beau replied in a weak voice. He raised an arm and waved.

Was he weak from hunger, boys both wondered, and how badly hurt?

"He's beat up good," Suzanne said, seeing the boys' expressions. "Are paramedics on the way?"

Boss Zimmerman stepped up to the cell. "Beau, I just have to apologize right now. I thought you'd jumped a train and left town. I'm sorry for ever doubting you."

"Mr. Z, I understand," the young man intoned softly. "I'm sorry to have caused you so much trouble."

Chief of Police Edward Jackson was soon beating a path up the old wooden stairs. He looked at his daughter and her best friend both locked behind bars and shook his head, scowling. "I'm sure there's an explanation for all this. There had better be." He shot another significant look at the two boys.

The mystery searchers introduced him to Beau.

Within minutes, a team of paramedics had streamed into the tiny space in front of the cell. However, getting through the barred steel door to give them access to the injured man proved difficult. The pirates had made off with the sole hundred-year-old key to the hundred-year-old lock.

"No problem," Boss Zimmerman declared.

He sent a welder off to the roundhouse. The man quickly returned with an acetylene cutting torch, a free-standing, battery-powered work light, and two other workers.

"Stand aside," said Boss Z.

One man turned on the lamp, which lit up the cell area like daylight. Another man fired up the blowtorch. The girls turned their backs and huddled in the corner, right next to Beau, as a shower of sparks rained down. The cell door proved no match for the torch. Within minutes, it had swung wide open.

"*Woo-hoo!*" Kathy shouted as the two girls stepped free. Suzanne hugged her father and the girls high-fived their brothers.

The paramedics stepped into the cell to assess Beau's condition before one of them addressed the waiting group. "He's got a fracture of his left forearm and severe facial lacerations and contusions. Plus he's sustained a serious loss of blood. Still, don't worry—we think he'll be fine in a couple of weeks. We just need to get him safe and sound in a nice hospital bed ASAP."

The two burliest paramedics gently transferred Beau to a stretcher and carried him down the stairs. The piercing sound of a siren penetrated the night before fading in the distance.

"I am *so* tired," Kathy said, glancing at her phone. It was after three in the morning. "But guess what? We now know exactly what the pirates were doing out here, don't we, Suzanne?"

The Chief issued a command. "Look, let's wrap things up for the night. I want everyone involved with this case to meet tomorrow morning at police headquarters. Ten o'clock, sharp—after we all get a little sleep. We'll all get debriefed and figure out what the heck happened out here."

He pulled Suzanne aside. "Call Beau's mother, pronto. I'll have an officer drive you to the hotel, then the hospital. Go."

Suzanne called Mrs. Bradley's room from her cell phone as she ran to the parking lot, which seemed full of police cars with the red lights whirling. "I'm sorry to wake you up so early, ma'am. This is Suzanne Jackson, and I have awfully great news for you."

"Beau's alive?"

"Yes, he sure is," Suzanne replied. "He needs medical attention, but the paramedics tell us he'll be just fine. Please get dressed and go downstairs. I'm coming in a squad car. We'll be waiting out front for you in about fifteen minutes." Suzanne heard background noise—a bed creaking, a light switch, water running.

"I'll be there. Is Beau in the hospital?"

"He's on his way in an ambulance now, and very eager to see you. We'll drive you right over."

Half an hour later, mother and son were reunited with joyful hugs. As she watched the drama play out in the emergency room, big tears rolled down Suzanne's cheeks.

20

THE PERFECT CRIME

A sizeable but exhausted—even *excited*—group trooped into Prescott's police headquarters on Monday morning at 10:00 a.m. The mystery searchers arrived first. Officers directed everyone to the station's training center, a facility large enough to handle the crowd.

People continued to trickle in. Joe and Maria Brunelli and the twins' mother, Sherri, arrived together. Boss Zimmerman and his secretary, Shirley, walked in next, soon followed by Fred Wilson. Shirley pulled out a large yellow pad, ready to take notes. A few interested police officers stood at the back of the room, and one of them escorted Mrs. Anita Bradley to the front row.

"We're ready," the Chief said. He began by introducing himself and the other officers. "Now where should we begin?"

"Let's start with Beau," Detective Ryan suggested. "How did he end up in that cell?"

Kathy spoke up. "Well, Beau explained the whole thing to"—she pointed a finger back and forth between herself and Suzanne—"us. The night he vanished, he had overheard a conversation between Hank Rogers and Billy Booker."

"Where?" Tom asked.

"Near the back of the roundhouse, where it's usually dark and deserted. Around seven in the evening, Beau had walked back in search of some replacement hardware. He overheard a snippet of hushed conversation between the two pirates, and they realized that he'd heard them talking. Something about counterfeit packaging. Unfortunately, Beau tripped as he backed away, which alerted the bad guys. They jumped poor Beau and dragged him out the rear exit door."

"That's where Jack Riley discovered his blood," Suzanne said with a frown. "Beau told us they beat the heck out of him."

"Why?" the Chief asked. "For what reason?"

Kathy explained, "That wasn't the first time they had a run-in with Beau. The same thing had happened a few nights earlier. One of the men referred to himself as a 'modern-day pirate,' and Beau picked up on it. He figured, 'Yup, these tough guys are thieves.' The next day, at the shift change, they warned him never to say a word to anyone—no matter what. Then, the night he vanished, they accused him of being a snitch."

The boys shot a knowing glance at one another. They recalled the aggressive scene they had witnessed in the security footage of the employee parking lot. It all made sense.

"How come they didn't bump him off?" Mr. Z asked. Only the night before, the boys had convinced him that Beau was deader than a doornail. Then everything changed.

"It wasn't their decision," Kathy replied. That startled everyone.

"Whose decision was it?" Mrs. Bradley asked.

"Ben Wright's," Suzanne replied.

People looked around the room. No sign of the man. In all the excitement, no one had even thought of the man.

The Chief asked, "What was *his* role?"

"Beau told us that Ben Wright was the ringmaster," Kathy replied flatly. "The pirates worked for him. They referred to him as 'Captain.'"

"Hang on," the Chief said. "Let's take this in order, or we'll all get lost. Officer Brady, does this square with what you learned?"

"Yes, Chief," she replied. She glanced over to Boss Zimmerman's secretary. "I need to back up a bit. Shirley posted an online ad for secretarial help. On Detective Ryan's orders, I interviewed and started the next day. As an undercover policewoman, my job was to vet the management."

"What does 'vet' mean?" Pete asked.

"It means to appraise them," Office Brady replied. "I had to separate truth from fiction and figure out who was acting in the best interests of the railroad."

"And to identify the pirates," Detective Ryan interjected.

"Keep going," the Chief prompted.

"Well, it became obvious that Boss Zimmerman and Shirley"—Officer Brady's eyes ticked around the room—"were in the clear. The finger of suspicion moved, thanks to Fred Wilson."

"Moved to whom?" Tom asked.

Officer Brady replied in a soft voice, "Ben Wright."

Mr. Z jumped in. "In fact, we owe a lot to Fred Wilson. Go ahead, Fred. Tell them."

Fred stood up, stammering, "I—I— Well, last Sunday night, just a few minutes before midnight, I noticed Hank Reynolds and Billy Booker sneaking around in the shadows. My first thought was, *That's strange, because their shift ended hours ago!* Both these guys are day-shift workers."

He paused for a second or two before continuing. "By then, I knew Deception Gap was under surveillance—last Friday I spotted Suzanne on the east hill, checking over the yard with binoculars. And I figured you all"—he glanced over at the mystery searchers and waved a hand at them—"were on the hunt for Beau Bradley . . . or what was left of him. That night I connected the dots and called the Jackson twins."

"What happened next?" Zimmerman urged.

The man nervously licked his lips. "The twins can answer that better than I." He sat down.

It was Tom's turn. "Suzie and I raced out to the yard. We watched the pirates—Reynolds and Booker—unlock a boxcar and swap out one box for another, both the same size. Later, we shot an image of the box they had stolen, covered with the logo for Simplicity Perfume, Singapore."

"Worth a fortune," Suzanne added.

The Chief asked, "Mr. Wilson, was that the first time these men came to your attention."

"Nope," Fred replied. He dutifully stood again. "I had spotted those lurkers two weeks back. They passed me driving toward Deception Gap as I headed home on the highway—after midnight, of course. I didn't think much about it—back then, Beau Bradley was alive and well. I figured they must have scheduled some over-time work. Then, I spotted you, Suzanne"—he pointed to her—"on the eastern summit. I realized that surveillance was taking place at Deception Gap."

"You called me to the tower Sunday morning," Mr. Z said. "Tell them what you said, Fred."

The training room fell quiet for a few seconds as everyone awaited Fred Wilson's words.

"I told you what the Jackson twins had witnessed the night before . . . that we had pirates operating at Deception Gap, and that the mystery searchers held the pirates responsible for Beau's disap-pearance. The shocker for me was that Ben Wright seemed to lead the operation."

Officer Brady jumped back into the conversation. "Mr. Z. shared that information with me, Chief. And I passed it on to Detective Ryan."

Suzanne thought back to their first meeting with Mr. Z and real-ized just how wrong she had been.

"Your surveillance program is the reason those pirates attacked you," Mr. Z said, nodding toward the mystery searchers. "If it hadn't been for Officer Brady, things might have turned out different-ly. She positioned us in a perfect location for a rescue."

The twins' mother, Sherri, coughed. Tom and Suzanne knew better than to glance over at her.

"Thank you, Mr. Zimmerman," the Chief said. "And excellent

job, Officer Brady." His eyes flicked over to the mystery searchers. "The pirates were waiting to attack you. How did they know you'd be there?"

"They didn't," Kathy replied. "The whole operation had blown up in their faces. Beau had turned into a real liability. . . Ben had disappeared, and so had their share of the spoils. . . plus they knew we were sneaking around, spying on them. They *hoped* we'd show—that we had answers—but when the boys escaped, they knew the game was up. They panicked."

"With no harm to you, I hope?" Mrs. Bradley piped up once more.

"Nope," Suzanne replied. "Just pushed us around and wanted to know where the boys might hide. We didn't have a clue. That's when they took off—in a hurry."

The Chief asked, "Have we figured out how the perfume scam worked?"

"Uh-huh," Kathy replied. "Beau listened to conversations among the pirates from behind bars. And Ben Wright shared info with him too."

"Beau told us," Suzanne said, "that the pirates began the piracy by breaking into one of the shipping containers and siphoning out twenty-five percent of the real perfume from each tiny bottle. That operation took a couple of hours."

"They would move the box to one of the abandoned outbuildings," Kathy said, "the ones near the old jail, to do the job without alerting the late-night crew They swapped out the stolen twenty-five percent with a formula Wright had cooked up."

Detective Ryan asked, "Any idea what the formula was?"

"According to what Ben Wright revealed to Beau," Kathy replied, "it included a tiny bit of distilled water and plain ethanol—cheap vodka, basically—which is odorless. Then the pirates repacked and sealed the altered perfume and sent it on its way."

"To its final destination," Kathy said. "And no one was any wiser."

"Because nothing seemed to be missing," Pete said. "Wow."

"Oh, man," Tom said. "I get it. If they do that three times and then use Wright's recipe to dilute it, they end up with a new boxful of two hundred and fifty bottles of the good stuff."

"Which would then generate," Detective Ryan said, completing the math, "a cool quarter million at black-market retail."

"Ben Wright told Beau all that?" the Chief asked.

"Yes, sir," Kathy replied. "Beau said Mr. Wright was quite proud of the operation."

Fred Wilson raised his hand with a question. "Where did they get the boxcar keys?"

"Ah, good question," Suzanne replied, her eyes searching the room. "We didn't ask about that."

"I can answer that," Detective Ryan declared. "We picked up the four pirates after Tom alerted me last night."

"Are they talking?" Pete asked.

"Three of them already lawyered up, but one of them—a guy named Alex Johnson—is singing like a bird. He told us that Ben Wright paid big bucks for a master set of keys stolen from the LA loading docks."

"That explains it," Tom said.

Shirley spoke up for the first time. "Who bought the counterfeit stuff?"

Kathy replied, "It went to the black market in New York. Even at discounted prices, and after the cut he gave the other pirates, Ben Wright made off with a fortune."

"Which explains why Tom and I spotted Rogers and Booker," Suzanne recalled, "hauling something out to the boxcar. They had a shipment of two hundred and fifty adulterated bottles ready to go; all they had to do was exchange it with the real thing."

"Correct," the Chief said. "And that's a five-minute operation. Darned ingenious."

"Any idea how big the total take was?" Pete asked. He had learned a lot of police language by hanging around the Jacksons.

"Johnson estimated two million," Detective Ryan replied.

Kathy shook her head, her long ponytail swinging back and

forth. "The perfect crime. No one had a clue anything was missing . . . because it wasn't."

"Wait a sec," Heidi said, trying to fill in one more blank. "The packaging for Simplicity Perfume looks darn unique—I checked it out online. How'd they get around that?"

"Ben Wright again," Kathy explained. "Remember, he told us he'd been a quartermaster for the army in South Korea. In that job, he worked with Korean factories—they manufactured parts and pieces for the U.S. Army. For a guy like Wright, this was an easy step—he knew the players, and who could handle the job. There are plenty of expert counterfeiters in Asia. Duplicate bottles, labels, ribbons, boxes, all the packaging—the works. Easy. The pirates even figured out a way to shrink-wrap the little boxes, both the original boxes they had to open, and the copies."

"And no questions asked," Suzanne summed up.

"Wouldn't anyone who bought a thousand-dollar bottle of fragrance know the difference?" Joe Brunelli asked.

"Well, you certainly wouldn't!" Maria cracked.

Laughter broke out around the room.

"Apparently not," the detective replied. "Simplicity Perfume told me it smelled almost identical and the replacement formula was undetectable—except to a chemist or a professional perfumer."

"Remember," Pete pointed out, "that the pirates were only skimming off twenty-five percent of the fragrance in each original bottle. And they diluted the perfume they stole by the exact same amount."

"Then along came an innocent Beau Bradley," Kathy said. "Without even knowing it, he lit the fuse that blew everything sky high."

21

A FRIEND INDEED

The following day, Heidi Hoover joined the mystery searchers as they crowded into Beau Bradley's tiny hospital room, each of them shaking his one good hand on the way in. His other arm rested in a sling, and a gauze bandage wrapped around his head.

Beau's mother rose from an easy chair, the kind that folded down into an uncomfortable bed. "I don't know how to thank you." She hugged each one of the mystery searchers as a tear rolled down her cheek, much to Pete's embarrassment. "But I don't know this young lady," she noted, looking to Heidi.

"This is our friend Heidi Hoover, the star reporter with *The Daily Pilot,*" Kathy said.

"Oh, yes," Mrs. Bradley said, "you wrote that story that helped flush the pirates into the open. Thank you so much, dear."

"No problem," Heidi replied. "Happy to be of assistance." She arched one eyebrow, looking wryly at her four young friends. A pen and notepad appeared from her pocket as she glanced over at the young man. "Do you prefer 'Beau' or 'Beauford'?" she asked.

Mrs. Bradley answered in a heartbeat. "That's Beauford," she said, looking over at Heidi's notepad. "Ending with a 'd.'"

Beau focused on the girls. "It must have been an awful shock when they threw you into the cell . . . and there I was."

Kathy giggled. "You got that right. In the dark, I didn't even see you. When you moved, I darn near freaked right out."

Suzanne said, "I couldn't wait to call your mother."

"How'd you get up there, anyway?" Pete wondered out loud.

"They carried me up," Beau answered, "like a sack of potatoes. Then they tossed me into that windowless cell, headfirst . . . and broke my arm. It's pitch-dark in there—I couldn't even see my own hand. It didn't take long to lose all sense of time. Plus, I kept blacking out. Every so often I called out for help, but the walls are so thick . . ."

He grinned at Heidi. "So you're the one who wrote that story on the Hutchinson family. That's where I found Kathy's cell phone number."

Heidi replied, "Yeah, and that was a mistake. The layout guys were supposed to make it disappear—to blur it out. We're not allowed-to publish phone numbers."

"Well, thank God for the error," he said.

"Amen," Mrs. Bradley said.

"One thing," Tom said, "that we've been wondering. All along, we figured the pirates had bumped you off."

"Especially when we found the blood out back," Kathy said. "But, of course, you're alive and well. How come?"

"Ben Wright," Beau answered.

"Ben Wright?" the mystery searchers chorused.

"Yup. He didn't want any part in a murder. In fact, he was furious when they beat me up—called all four of them 'Neanderthals'—plus other things I'd blush to repeat. Brought me food and water every day and even told me when the jig was up . . . the day before he just stopped coming." He grinned. "Even brought me extra rations and said goodbye."

"By 'they,' you mean Rogers and Booker?" Suzanne asked.

"Yeah, and their two buddies. I had never met Johnson or the other guy, although I'd seen them working in the yard. Believe me, if the four of them had had their way—and if you four hadn't come along just in time—I'd be a dead duck by now."

His mother made the sign of the cross.

"When they catch Ben—*if* they catch him—I'll be testifying on his behalf," Beau continued. "He saved my life." He paused for a few seconds. "And so did you."

Murmurs of "No, no, not at all . . ." ran around the bed.

A thought crossed Tom's mind. "It's interesting that the chief pirate, Ben Wright—they called him 'Captain'—had a conscience. When we think of piracy today, it's all about software or technology piracy. But these guys were stealing real merchandise. I wonder how they came up with the piracy moniker?"

"I'm not sure," Beau replied. "First time I heard it, the word came out of Rogers's mouth. But it sure was appropriate, wasn't it?"

Kathy had a question. "Ben Wright disappeared the night of the box exchange we saw. Why?"

"Greed, I'd guess," Beau replied. "My understanding was that he *never* showed up to do the physical work, and that included the exchanges. But that night he told the pirates he was coming. It ended up that he threw the box of real stuff into his SUV and headed out for parts unknown. Those pirates weren't real happy with him—or you."

"No wonder," Tom said. "He had just ripped his partners off."

"And hung them out to dry," Pete added.

Just then, a shy Jack Riley trudged into the room without realizing he was stepping into the middle of a small crowd. He tried to back out.

"No way, Jack!" Heidi crowed at him. "You get back in here right now!"

Before he uttered a word, Kathy walked up and hugged him. "Jack, that was you who warned us, wasn't it?"

As usual, his eyes whipped around the room, searching for an escape—this time from Kathy. "Yeah . . . yeah, well, that was me. Someone yelled 'Intruders!' I guessed that might be you."

Pete stuck his hand out. "I'm Kathy's brother. Thank you, Jack. We owe you."

"No sweat," he muttered, shaking the outstretched hand. He glanced over at Beau. "I'm glad you're okay, man."

"Thanks, Jack."

Soon enough, Heidi—with another story for the front page—waved goodbye and headed out. She dragged Jack along with her. The mystery searchers said their goodbyes too and trailed behind.

"You think they'll ever catch Ben Wright?" Suzanne asked.

"You never know," Heidi replied.

Tom had confidence in the department. "Prescott City Police figures he's toast, that's for sure."

"I dunno," Pete figured. "That scam made him wealthy. He could hide anywhere in the world. He might have caught a flight before the APB went out for his arrest . . ."

"Or driven across the border to Mexico," Tom said.

"All the money in the world won't help when they put those handcuffs on him," Kathy figured out loud.

Suzanne demurred. "Just imagine: the guy wronged by the crime offered to testify in favor of the ringmaster. That's a first!"

EPILOGUE

The vanishing at Deception Gap yielded a handful of happy endings. Beau Bradley soon recovered from his injuries—with a little help from his mom—and returned to work. Boss Zimmerman talked him into staying on at the railyard; in fact, he made Beau a foreman and raised his salary.

Two months later, Beau's mother sold her home in Philadelphia and relocated to Prescott. "Nicest place I ever visited," she claimed to friends back in Philly. "Did you know the city is home to the world's oldest rodeo?" She purchased an older house close to downtown. Beau moved in with her. Days later, she applied for an Arizona real estate license.

Heidi Hoover's Deception Gap stories hit the front page two days in a row, making heroes out of two of her favorite people, Beau Bradley and Jack Riley.

Simplicity Perfume rewarded Beau with ten bottles of their renowned brand. He distributed them to all the delighted women now in his life: his mom, Heidi, Suzanne and Kathy and their mothers, and a handful of nurses at Prescott Regional Hospital.

"I mean, c'mon, perfume?" he joked when the shipment arrived. "What the heck am I gonna to do with the stuff?"

"No problem," Kathy said with a giggle. She dabbed a touch on her neck. "This stuff is heavenly. Call me if they send more."

Romance blossomed too. One night, two months later, the foursome attended a play at Prescott's renowned Opera House.

Suzanne spotted them first and nudged Kathy. "Do you see what I see?"

In the very front row, Heidi Hoover and Beau Bradley sat side by side. Close too.

"That's so sweet!" Kathy stammered.

Pete yawned.

Ben Wright, the man who had masterminded the perfect crime, had disappeared. An outstanding warrant is still open for his arrest. Detective Ryan believes it's only a matter of time before Mr. Wright sees the inside of Arizona State Prison.

"And all of it—*everything*," Kathy quipped, "happened because of Beauford Bradley's love for the Old West."

EXCERPT FROM BOOK 7

The Heist Forgotten by Time

Chapter 1

Surprise!

Suzanne nosed the late-model Chevy Impala into a gravel parking lot at Watson Lake, a popular hiking destination just north on highway 89. It was morning, not long after eight o'clock, two days after Christmas.

The twins stepped out into a bracing wind that whirled dead leaves in their path. Dark, threatening clouds scudded past at a furious pace. Before them, acres of blue-grey water glinted as whitecaps raced across the lake's surface. Somewhere in the distance, birds screeched. . . a warning, perhaps, of a coming storm. Or worse.

"Suzie, you picked a wonderful morning for a hike," Tom grumbled. He raised his hand into the wind, feeling for droplets of rain.

Nothing. . . yet. He glanced up. "Those clouds could hammer us at a moment's notice."

"Lovely. Couldn't be better." She took a deep breath. Indeed, it smelled like rain. And trees. And fresh air, all mingled together in a delightful, outdoorsy fragrance.

The shoreline—punctuated by huge, rounded granite boulders, many of them semi-submerged—extended out into narrow promontories flanked by tiny islands. In some places, boulders rose majestically, almost cliff-like, from the water's edge. Barren aspen trees, scattered around the lake, bent in the heady gusts.

In the rustic beauty that lay before them, *isolated* and *lonely* were words that sprang to mind. But *danger?* No. Not at all.

"Can you believe it?" Suzanne wondered out loud. "Not another car in sight—we'll have the trail to ourselves." The wind shifted in a sudden burst, pushing her long brown ponytail aside. She zipped up the Christmas gift from her parents—a fleece-lined dark-blue jogging suit. Warm as toast.

"Okay by me," Tom said. He pulled on a weather-breaker jacket, snug and water-resistant—*just in case*—setting his mind to the task at hand. "Let's go." A canteen rested over one shoulder as he angled left, pushing hard into the headwind.

A five-mile hiking trail, guided by white dots along the pathway, circled a lake situated one mile above sea level. The better part of the pathway remained flat before climbing into a moderate hike that twisted and turned around the enormous boulders.

"Nice," Suzanne noted. "They shelter us from the wind."

At one stage, Tom turned and called out to his sister. "Careful, Suzie. The path is slippery on this rocky surface." A recent dusting of snow had all but disappeared. It had arrived early Christmas morning, melting away by noon the following day—Boxing Day— leaving a chill in the air and a healthy wind that gusted strong and often.

They trudged onward in silence, each bend revealing Watson Lake's hidden secrets. Fifteen minutes passed before something on the ground caught Tom's eye, stopping him dead. He fell to one knee.

"What is it?" Suzanne asked.

"Mountain lion tracks."

"Oh, joy." She bent over beside him and peered straight down. "Yup, you're right. Fresh ones too."

The twins' experiences in rugged central Arizona—they were born and raised in Prescott—left no doubt. A mountain lion's paw print, front or rear, displays a distinctive triangular heel surrounded by four clawed toes. The top of the heel has two lobes, while the bottom has three. The elongated toes are like extended ovals.

In the soft, wet earth, the tracks were a perfect match for the illustration they remembered vividly from their childhood Scouting manual.

Not to mention previous hikes—central Arizona *is* mountain lion country. And every so often. . .

Tom stood. "Okay, as long as we stick together, the cat won't bother us." They set off again, this time with a touch of apprehension.

A quarter mile later, they rounded a curve just in time to spot a silent, tawny-colored flash of fur whip from one side of the trail to the other. Fifty yards at most.

"What the heck—" Tom started. He came to a complete stop. "Did you see that tail?"

"It's the mountain lion," Suzanne hissed. "And he's hiding between those two boulders."

"Serious?"

"Serious."

The twins knew attacks on humans were rare. And two people hiking together? Never. Still . . .

Tom flapped his arms in the air. Mountain lions attack when their prey is small, but size and noise frighten them. *"Beat it!"* he yelled.

"Oh . . . my . . . gosh," Suzanne uttered. "I can barely see it . . .

look, behind the boulders, on the other side of that bush. It's watching us!"

"Never run from a mountain lion," Tom murmured. That adage —drilled into them since childhood—had popped into his mind.

"Back away . . . easy," Suzanne urged. "If there's any movement, scream."

"Boys don't scream."

"Try."

The twins edged backward, ever so slowly.

Then, seemingly out of nowhere—*so sudden, so fast*—a medium-sized dog rushed from behind them, brushing past as it beelined over to the mountain lion. The dirty white mongrel with gray splotches stopped a few yards before the boulders—the cat's head, ears straight back, was only just visible—barking and growling, loud and menacing. It paced in a semicircle, never taking its eyes off the predator.

Seconds later, the dog quit barking. The mountain lion had, it appeared, backed off. Gone.

"Dang!" Tom exclaimed.

Suzanne breathed again. It was over, thank God. The mongrel turned and approached the twins, warily.

To be continued. . .

I hope you have enjoyed this sneak peek at book 7 in The Mystery
Searchers Family Book Series

The Heist Forgotten by Time

To be released Fall, 2020

BIOGRAPHY

Barry Forbes began his writing career in 1980, eventually scripting and producing hundreds of film and video corporate presentations, winning a handful of industry awards along the way. At the same time, he served as an editorial writer for Tribune Newspapers and wrote his first two books, both non-fiction.

In 1997, he founded and served as CEO for Sales Simplicity Software, a market leader which was sold two decades later.

What next? "I always loved mystery stories and one of my favorite places to visit was Prescott, Arizona. It's situated in rugged central Arizona with tremendous locales for mysteries." In 2017, Barry merged his interest in mystery and his skills in writing, adding in a large dollop of technology. The Mystery Searchers Family Book Series was born.

Barry's wife, Linda, passed in 2019 and the series is dedicated to her. "Linda proofed the initial drafts of each book and acted as my chief advisor." The couple had been married for 49 years and had two children. A number of their fifteen grandchildren provided feedback on each book.

Contact Barry: barry@mysterysearchers.com

Book 5: The Treasure of Skull Valley

Suzanne discovers a map hidden in the pages of a classic old book at the thrift store. It's titled "My Treasure Map" and leads past Skull Valley, twenty miles west of Prescott and into the high desert country—to an unexpected, shocking and elusive treasure. "Please help," the note begs. The mystery searchers utilize the power and reach of the Internet to trace the movement of people and events. . . half a century earlier.

Book 6: The Vanishing in Deception Gap

A text message to Kathy sets off a race into the unknown. "There are pirates operating out here and they're dangerous. I can't prove it, but I need your help." Who sent the message? Out where? Pirates! How weird is that? The mystery searchers dive in, but it might be too late. *The man has vanished into thin air.*

Book 7: The Heist Forgotten by Time

Coming – Fall/Winter, 2020

Don't forget to check out
www.MysterySearchers.com

Register to receive *free* parent/reader study guides for each book in the series—valuable teaching and learning tools for middle-grade students and their parents.

You'll also find a wealth of information on the website: stills and video scenes of Prescott, reviews, press releases, awards, and more. Plus, I'll update you on new book releases and other news.